A LETTER TO MAMA AND OTHER UNCOLLECTED STORIES

A LETTER TO MAMA AND OTHER UNCOLLECTED STORIES

ISAAC BASHEVIS SINGER

Goodreads Press

TABLE OF CONTENTS

INTRODUCTION

Of the hundreds of short stories that Isaac Bashevis Singer published in the Yiddish press and literary journals during his life, he translated, published, and collected nearly two hundred in twelve separate collections – starting with *Gimpel the Fool and Other Stories* (1958) and ending with *The Death of Methuselah and Other Stories* (1988). Even this did not reflect the full extent of his output. When he published his self-selected anthology, *Collected Stories* (1982) – consisting of 45 stories translated and published in English until that point in time – he included five *uncollected* stories among the ones that had already appeared in book form. Given the inevitable page limits involved in such an undertaking, this meant leaving out at least as many worthy stories as were included. When Ilan Stavans edited the Library of America's three-volume *Collected Stories* in 2004, he included thirteen additional stories translated in Singer's lifetime and found in his archive, but never published or collected in English— bringing the total stories in that publication to over two hundred. This still did not exhaust the extent of Singer's creative output. Beyond the tens of stories that remain untranslated, about a dozen translated during his lifetime remained unpublished.

I began working with Singer's papers at the Harry Ransom Center rather accidentally – when, during my doctoral research,

I came upon, "Job," a story that was published and collected in Yiddish under its original title, "Iyev," but which never appeared in English. After translating the story as part of my research and arranging to publish it in *The New Yorker* – which had published over sixty stories by Singer during his lifetime – I checked the finding aid to look for another document and noticed an entry in the section marked "Unidentified works" that described the same character as the one named in "Job." I ordered a facsimile of that fragment and found that it was a translation of the same story, made by Singer and Dorothea Straus, the wife of Singer's publisher, Roger Straus. I incorporated elements of that translation into my own into the version published in *The New Yorker* in 2012. Yet just as the story appeared, I found a separate entry in the unidentified section that also reflected elements of the story, and after I received those pages, realized that the *entire* story had been translated but then relegated to the unidentified section, apparently because the first page was missing. This raised a question that has been raised repeatedly around Singer's unpublished works in general, and about his unpublished short stories in particular. Why weren't they published while he was still alive?

There are at least two directions from which this question should be addressed, the first being *quantity*, and the second being *quality*.

Singer composed an unbelievable *quantity* of text – not all of which has been published even in Yiddish – and has been regarded by some as an overrated graphomaniac: a compulsive writer. Singer, as usual, was aware of this accusation, and even discussed the concept in a memoir series published in the *Forverts* as *Figurn un epizodn fun fun literatn farayn* (1979-1980), which was excerpted in English translation in *Kesher*, an Israeli journal, just months after Singer's death in 1991. The excerpt appeared as "Images and Episodes from the Writers' Association House in Warsaw: Memoirs of Bashevis Singer, Apprentice Journalist," and in that piece, Singer writes:

> I've mentioned graphomania and graphomaniacs before. These are concepts rarely used in English, but frequently used in European languages. The Europeans believe that writing can sometimes become a madness. Actually, the entire civilized world suffers from this madness. There is also a question as to whether it can be defined as a malady. The lust for writing is identical with the need to speak, to communicate. The pen or the typewriter do exactly what the mouth, the tongue, and the lips did thousands of years ago: convey thoughts and feelings, mostly expressions of disappointment, fantasies, and dreams. If speaking is not a madness, then neither is writing.

Singer might have been a compulsive communicator, but he was also recognized as a master storyteller. His mastery came not only from inborn talent, but also from edits and revisions. He was an artist of variations, too, so what any given story can communicate to us is revealed not only by the apparent words or narrative, but also by how it is different from other, similar narratives Singer had composed. From the perspective of literary history and the issue of quantity in a writer's life, this gives reading his stories at least two dimensions. Readers less familiar with Singer's writing can enjoy the narratives for their storytelling mastery. Readers more familiar with Singer's writing have the privilege of seeing how he winds the threads of his narrative in different directions even when the circumstances seem similar to stories he has written before. Criticizing Singer for having already written some version of a story is like critiquing Bach for composing thirty variations of a single aria just so that he and

Johann Gottlieb Goldberg could show off what could be done with a piano. It undervalues the pleasure of the familiar as well as the power of nuance while over-privileging the new, unknown, and unfamiliar.

As for *quality*, this, too, raises an ongoing debate, especially when posthumously publishing the works of an internationally recognized writer like Singer. In the case of most writers, the first measure is whether the writer intended to publish the given work, or whether it is simply something left behind, unfinished and unpolished, and is now being touted as having unrecognized value. In Singer's case, these questions are complicated by the publication history of his work, as well as the labor-intensive process of bringing out his writings in English, which became not only a question of translation but, in Singer's case, part and parcel of the writing process. In Singer's lifetime, any given story usually went through three or four stages before it was collected in English. It was first written longhand in Yiddish, only sometimes typed up with light edits, and sent to the *Forverts* or some Yiddish literary journal for final editing and publication. After this, it was chosen by Singer for translation, which was usually done with a collaborator though later alone, and went through several edits and versions that Singer would correct in English. It was then sent to an agent to be placed in a magazine, a long process involving waiting for responses to submissions and, when accepted, additional edits and corrections. Only much later, sometimes years after first appearing in translation, were the stories finally chosen among a pool of publications to be collected in book form—a process which itself depended on practical parameters like projected page counts and price points. It is inevitable that, in a process with so many steps, some stories intended for publication fell by the wayside, not because of their quality, but because the process was so long and complicated. Add to this the issue of new stories being produced all the time, we well as the limitations of a publisher releasing so much material by a single author, and you have a situation in which stories of solid literary quality are set aside because of other considerations.

These other considerations sometimes also had to do with thematic concerns, particularly how a story's subject might be received during the cultural climate of the moment, as well as Singer's public persona and the type of work associated with him. In terms of themes, it is worth noting the degree to which death factors as a theme in many of these stories, not as an event told after the fact, but in terms of its effect on those who survive. Whether told as a ghost story, the report of a man's consciousness as it passes from life to death, or a dying man's fantasy of being reunited with his mother's spirit, many of these stories explore the ubiquitous presence of death in our everyday lives. In terms of Singer's public literary identity, some of these stories show a more experimental side of his work, placing himself in the story as author like Vladimir Nabokov or Kurt Vonnegut, or else presenting a story in the form of a dialogue without exposition, as William Gaddis and, some time later, Philip Roth did. But unlike these writers, who were known as postmodern experimenters with literary structure, Singer's reputation was built on his public image as an old-fashioned storyteller. Some scholars, like David Neal Miller and David Roskies, focused on Singer's ability to undermine genre expectations through what Roskies calls "creative betrayal"—but the extent of his literary experimentation, which can be found in many of his untranslated pieces, has not been fully appreciated. Some of these stories, which were published in his lifetime, appeared in magazines like *Playboy*, *Newsday*, *The Jewish Chronicle*, *The Critic*, and *Israel Magazine*—which were less literary than magazines like *The Atlantic*, *Harper's*, or *The New Yorker*, but which all published high-quality fiction.

The current collection brings together stories that were translated in Singer's lifetime but left uncollected or unpublished. The years in which I started working with Singer's papers coincided with the establishment of the Isaac Bashevis Singer Literary Trust, created by Singer's grandchildren in memory of their father, Singer's only child, the Israeli writer and journalist Israel Zamir. The Singer Literary Trusts's efforts have focused, among other things, on publishing stories translated by Singer or under his personal supervision, which appeared in *The New Yorker, Harper's Magazine, Paris Review, Tablet, Narrative, Jewish Review of Books*, and *American Scholar* in the recent years. While publishing these stories, my research on Singer's life and work brought to my attention a number of stories that were published in Singer's lifetime but remained uncollected. As a collection of stories translated by Singer, their order, too, is arranged according to his approach, alternating between different storytelling approaches, settings, and themes, aiming to create an arc that gives readers a sense of variety as they proceed throughout the collection as a whole.

Regarding translation, it should be noted that, while Singer used young unexperienced people to help translate his work, most of them didn't know Yiddish and worked more as stenographers. Some of the exceptions included Joseph Singer, the son of Israel Joshua Singer and Singer's nephew, Mirra Ginsburg, a seasoned translator from several languages, and Aliza Shevrin, who is today known for her translations of Sholem Aleichem. In many cases, the final works were signed, "Translated by the author and __________," giving the name of the person who served as collaborator. Singer never admitted in writing that he translated himself, but he did address the issue after a lecture about the craft of writing. The sound recording, stored at the Ransom Center, was made on January 29, 1964, and in response to a question on translating his stories, he answers:

> I write everything in Yiddish, but I translate them myself lately. I used to have translators, but now I do a lot of

> the translation myself. I translate word by word, and I have a collaborator who helps me organize the sentences so that they should sound more English. Because in my case I know the words, but I don't know the construction of the English sentence so well as a man who was born here.

In this collection, all translators are credited as they appeared in the published or typescript versions. In the cases where no translator is listed, Singer is credited alone for the translation, though this does not rule out the possibility of an uncredited collaborator. Still, all typescripts—without exception—exhibit Singer's original hand-written corrections in the English language, suggesting that the credit for the final versions indeed lies with the author. The only story that has a different translation history in this collection is "Job," which appears here in a slightly different version from the one that was published in *The New Yorker*, taking into consideration most of Singer's original translation, integrating his choices with mine in what amounts to a posthumous three-way collaboration credited as translated by the author, Dorothea Straus, and myself. As for bibliographic history, which can be found in full at the back of this collection, most of these stories first appeared in the Yiddish press, with the exception of several that were translated into English but have no known Yiddish publication.

These stories—the ones published in Singer's lifetime and the ones published in recent years—all underwent an additional round of editing in preparation for this collection. The driving principle behind these efforts is that the posthumous publication of Singer's work is neither merely a question of finding hidden treasures, nor publishing his literary leftovers for the sake of posterity, but rather that it is a reestablishment of Singer's "business as usual"—picking up where Singer left off when he passed away, and finishing the work of translating, editing, and publishing his full literary legacy.

As a final note, I would like to stress that everything discussed in this preface relates to Singer's *translated but uncollected or unpublished material*—not only these short stories, but also novels and a partially translated memoir. And this does not even begin to address the issue of his untranslated work—including the cultural criticism he published on a regular basis for decades, and the additional novels, stories, and memoirs that he did not have a chance to translate before his death in 1991. Beyond the essays, novels, stories, and memoirs translated in his lifetime, there are approximately thirty additional stories, seven novellas, eight novels, and several volumes of autobiographical series that are accessible only in the original Yiddish—without taking into account the hundreds of articles and reviews he wrote as an arts and culture journalist. This collection marks one in a set of concerted undertakings, already begun in Europe with the release of several unpublished novels and in the United States with the translation and publication of his wartime writings for the *Forverts*, to bring out the rest of Singer's corpus. The work is underway, and there is a long literary road yet to be traveled before the full extent of Singer's literary achievement is known to the community of global readers.

—David Stromberg, Jerusalem

THE BOARDER

Outside, there was the rumbling of a truck that wouldn't start. It rattled and gasped as if its metal soul were about to expire. Children were playing baseball and screaming wildly. The air coming through the open window smelled of gasoline, scallions, and the beginning of summer. Around the ceiling light, a swarm of flies eddied, droning monotonously. Through the window, hung with Dutch curtains, a butterfly flew in and landed on the table. It stood motionless, its wings together, waiting with the fatalistic calm of a creature that lives for only a short time. Reb Berish Zhichliner, in prayer shawl and phylacteries, had already finished his proper prayers, but he kept on reciting additional supplications, which are repeated only by the very pious and by those who have a lot of time.

Reb Berish's beard was white, and his face was red. He had bushy brows, and double bags hanging under his eyes. It had been only two years since he retired from his business in fabric remnants. For forty years, he'd had a pushcart on the Lower East Side, and also here in Williamsburg. His wife, his son, and a daughter had died during this time. Another daughter was living with a Gentile husband somewhere in California. Nothing was left to Reb Berish except his pension, a grave site in the cemetery that belonged to the Sochaczew Society, and an apartment on Clymer Street. In order not to live alone, he'd taken in a refugee as a boarder, a man who'd come back from the camps, spent time in Soviet Russia, and then wandered through half the world. His name was Morris Melnik. He contributed fifteen dollars a month toward the rent. At the moment, he was still sleeping in his room, which had a window that gave onto a fire escape.

Reb Berish had taken him in more out of pity than for the fifteen dollars. Morris Melnik had lost everything: his parents, his sisters and brothers, his wife, and his child. Still, Reb Berish regretted ever having opened his home. Melnik was a mocker and an unbeliever, a lecher, a contrary creature. He tried monkey business with the neighborhood women. He mixed meat and milk dishes. He came home at two o'clock in the morning and slept until a little before noon. He didn't pray, didn't observe the Sabbath. Just as Reb Berish began to recite the Thirteen Principles of Faith, Melnik entered the room: a little man whose face was yellowed as if by jaundice and whose head bore only a few stray strands of black and gray hair. He wore red pajamas and shabby slippers. He hadn't yet shaved, and there were black shadows on his sunken cheeks. He had a pointed chin, a thin bony nose. His small eyes were hidden behind long, needle-like eyebrows. He reminded Reb Berish of a hedgehog. When he opened his mouth, he revealed a line of teeth studded with gold fillings. He said, "Are you still praying, Reb Berish?"

"Well . . . "

"To whom are you praying? To the God who made Hitler and gave him the strength to kill six million Jews? Or perhaps to the God who created Stalin and let him liquidate another ten million victims? Really, Reb Berish, you're not going to bribe the Lord of the Universe with a pair of phylacteries. He's a first-class son of a bitch and a terrible anti-Semite."

"*Pfui.*" Reb Berish grimaced. "Go away."

"How long will we keep cringing before Him and singing Psalms?" Melnik continued. "I've seen with my very own eyes how they threw a Jew with a prayer shawl and phylacteries into a ditch full of shit. Literally."

Reb Berish's red face turned even redder. He was in a hurry to finish the Articles of the Creed so that he could answer his lodger. He murmured, "I believe in perfect faith that there will be a resurrection of the dead at a time when it shall please the Creator. Blessed be His name, and exalted be the remembrance of Him forever and ever." He closed the prayer book but left his index finger inside, so that he could open it again at the same spot after he'd given Melnik a proper answer. He sighed and grumbled.

"Will you stop blaspheming? I don't tell you how to behave, and don't you try to teach me. No matter what you've seen, the Almighty is still a merciful God. We don't know His ways. If we knew Him, we'd be like Him. Free choice was granted to us, and that's that. Those who threw that Jew into the filth will never leave Gehenna, and his blessed soul will rest at the Throne of Glory."

"Nonsense. Empty words. Where is the soul? There is no soul, Reb Berish. It was invented by idlers in the study house. In Russia, there was a Professor Pavlov, and he was the greatest of them all. A real big shot, as they say in America. He cut out the brains of a dog and he found no soul there. A brain is a machine, just like in an automat. You throw in three nickels and out comes a sandwich. The machine doesn't need your nickels. You can put in wooden slugs. It was just made that way, and nothing else."

"You compare a saintly man to a dog or an automat. You should be ashamed of yourself, Mr. Melnik. A machine is a machine, and man is created in the image of God."

"The image of God! I sat in the Moscow prison in a cell with the Rabbi of Bludnov. For seven weeks, we sat together, and in all that time he did one thing: studied the Torah. He suffered from hemorrhoids, and when he sat on the chamber pot he bled like an animal. In the middle of the night, they'd wake him up and take him for an interrogation. I could hear him screaming, and when he returned he couldn't walk anymore. They pushed him into the cell, and he fell down on the floor. We revived him as best we could. After seven weeks of torture, they took him out one night to be shot."

"Well, so did he protest about God's injustice?"

"No, he remained a believer until his last breath."

Reb Berish winced and rubbed his forehead. "When free choice is given, free choice is given. It means that the wicked have the power to do wickedness as they please. Does the government here on earth not give free choice? Every gangster can kill, steal, rob until he's caught. But when he's caught he gets his due."

"The Nazis didn't get their due, Reb Berish. I was in Munich after the war. They were all sitting in a huge beer hall, red and fat like pigs, swilling beer and singing Nazi songs with wild voices. They boasted openly about how many Jews they'd burned, gassed, buried alive, and about how many Jewish girls they'd raped. You should have heard their laughter. America was sending them billions of dollars, and they poured the Bayerisches down their gullets and gobbled their *Weisswurst*. Their paunches almost burst with pleasure. When I entered, and they recognized that I was a Jew, they became like beasts. They wanted to finish me off right on the spot."

"Why did you go into such a place?"

"I had a German girlfriend there. I smuggled gold and she hid it. We worked, as they say, fifty-fifty. And we had another business besides."

"*Pfui*, you're no better than they are."

"What could I do? The Jewish girls were all sick and bitter. When you lay down with them, they did nothing but complain until your ears popped. All they wanted was to get married and settle down. But not me. With a German girl, you got what you wanted, without any fuss. For a pack of American cigarettes, you could have had Himmler's widow."

"Do me a favor and keep quiet. If you're not going to let me pray in peace, be so good as to move out of the house. We're not a good match."

"Don't scold me, Reb Berish. As far as I'm concerned, you can pray from morning until evening. Keep on flattering God, tell Him how great He is, how good, how merciful, and He'll prepare a second Hitler for you. They're already preparing. America's sending them airplanes. One day they'll give them the atomic bomb, too. On your taxes, Reb Berish, Germany is being rearmed. This is the truth."

Reb Berish clutched his beard. "This is not the whole truth yet. Please, go back to your room, and let me continue with my prayers."

"Continue, continue. The one who begrudges you should grow a horn on his belly."

After prayers, Reb Berish began to rummage around the kitchen and prepare breakfast. Actually, it was a combination of breakfast and lunch, because Reb Berish ate only two meals a day. He rummaged and sighed. The doctor had forbidden everything he liked: salt, pepper, sauerkraut, radishes, mustard, herring, pickles, even butter and sour cream. What was left? Toast with farmer's cheese and a cup of weak tea. He could have eaten spinach or cauliflower, but he would never get used to that kind of food. Even the fruit in America didn't have the old home taste. The truth was that since his wife, Feige Malke, died, everything had lost its taste and its sense: going to bed, getting up in the morning, receiving a check from Uncle Sam, even the Sabbaths and holy days. Reb Berish had many times made up his mind not to have any more conversations with his boarder, the charlatan who had gone through hell and remained no good. But sitting alone at the table was also hard. Somehow this grumbling boarder's harsh words took the place of onion, horseradish, garlic, or a glass of vodka. They made his heart beat faster, heated the blood in his veins. Reb Berish called out, "Hey, Mr. Melnik, come and have a cup of tea."

Melnik immediately appeared at the door. He'd combed the hair over his bald spot and smeared it with pomade. He wore a pink shirt, a yellow tie with black dots, a pair of khaki Army pants, and Army shoes that one could buy cheaply. On the ring finger of his left hand, he wore a signet ring with a ruby, and around his wrist a watch with a gold band. In his shirt pocket, he had three fountain pens and two pencils with silver tops. After shaving and taking a bath, he seemed somehow younger. The bags under his eyes had flattened out. His eyes had become clearer. Reb Berish looked at him in amazement.

"Well, have something."

"What shall I have? If you had prepared such a table in the camps, it would have been something. I was there when they killed a Jew because he stole a potato. He was a relative of mine. There was a fellow in our camp who had a store. You can imagine what a store this was. He kept his merchandise in the bunk where he slept. If he had been caught, he would have been shot immediately. He would have been lucky if they shot him. They probably would have tortured him. But business is business. I've seen Jews martyred for business. So it was in the ghettos, and so it was in Russia. Because of a few spools of thread and a dozen needles, people were condemned to death. In the camps, such a merchant kept a few leaves of cabbage, some potato peels, and some wilted radishes: that was his trade. But hunger is a bitter thing. In the Russian camps, people got sick with scurvy, from a lack of vitamins. One dies from these sicknesses quite suddenly. I saw it happen once."

"Wait a moment, Mr. Melnik. Better take a slice of bread with cheese. Have some cherries."

"Thank you. I was lying on my bunk one winter night, somewhere in a camp in Kazakhstan, talking with my neighbor on the bunk across from me. It was so cold the water in the pail froze. We covered ourselves with all our rags. Outside, the frost was terrible. We were hungry, too, but we talked. What did we talk about? About wives and children who stayed with the Germans, and about the good old times, and what we would do when peace came again. We were going to do only one thing – eat. We pictured all the roasts and cakes we'd put away, the chicken soup with noodles, the stuffed derma, the onions in chicken fat, the schnitzels and cutlets. For a while, it was quiet. Then I asked my neighbor something, but he didn't answer. Did he fall asleep? I asked myself. And I listened. Usually, he snored, because he had polyps in his nose, but now he was strangely quiet. I slid down the bunk to take a look. The man was dead. One second he was talking, the next he was dead."

"Terrible, terrible."

"What are you crying for? This is humanity, the crown of creation. My theory is that all men are Nazis. What right do we have to slaughter a calf and eat it? The one with the knife slaughters. It's just as Hitler believed: might is right. As for God, He's a Nazi to end all Nazis. The arch-Hitlerite. He has more power than anybody else, so He tortures everybody. You see, I'm not an unbeliever. There is a Gehenna, there is. Why should people suffer only on earth? They're tortured in the hereafter, too. God has His own Treblinka, with devils, hobgoblins, demons, angels of death. They burn the poor sinners or hang them by their tongues or by their breasts. All the details are there in 'The Rod of Punishment.' But there's no paradise. When it comes to death, I become a real heretic."

Reb Berish stopped chewing. "Why would the Creator of the world be so cruel?"

"Why wouldn't He be? He's got the big stick, so He uses it. He's given us a Torah, which nobody can keep. Each little rabbi adds new laws, and if you break one of these laws you're reincarnated as a snake. The Christians maintain that God could not redeem mankind until He let His only son die on the Cross. One way or another, all He demands is blood."

"Well, better eat something. Too much talk only leads to iniquity."

"I'm eating. What else am I doing? The only thing that's left for me is eating. The women here in America are no good. The truth is that there are no more good women anywhere. In my time, there were still some faithful wives. Nowadays, that species has disappeared altogether. If you had seen what I saw, your white beard would have turned black again."

"I don't want to hear about it."

"I'm not talking about the camps. There a woman couldn't help herself. When one is afraid for one's life, one will do anything. I once heard a mother persuading her daughter to give herself to a scabby Ukrainian man because he could put more groats in her bowl of soup. She actually did it, and, when the Nazis learned about it, all three of them were murdered. Such events did not leave much of an impression – we became accustomed to them. But I witnessed even worse things. After we were freed, nobody was forced anymore, but they still wallowed in filth. We slept three families to a room. In one corner, a woman fornicated with a peasant, and in the other corner her sister did the same. They lost all sense of shame. They deloused themselves together and they fornicated together. One liked to do it by candlelight."

"Will you keep quiet or not? I'm warning you for the last time."

"Are you afraid of the truth?"

"This is not the truth. Sin is like froth. When you pour beer into a glass, you imagine that it's full, but two-thirds of it is froth. When the froth dissolves, only a third of the glass is left. The same thing is true of transgressions. They burst like bubbles."

"Well said. Is this your own thought?"

"I heard it from our rabbi."

"A nice saying, but I say that everything is filth. Nothing is real but filth. Your rabbi is also filth. Behind his beard and his sidelocks and the fringed garment is a man who loves females, and if he weren't married to a good-looking woman he would run to whores."

"Rascal! Betrayer of Israel!"

"Rascal, shmascal. I don't say that I'm a saint. I do anything I can. So what do you want from me? By the way, why don't you remarry? You're still healthy. I wouldn't leave you alone with a Gentile woman for a minute."

Reb Berish groaned. He set a fist on the table. With his other hand, he picked the crumbs from his beard. "Nonsense! You say the meanest things about women, but my Feige Malke, peace be with her, was a pious woman. She wouldn't even look at another man. She was just like my mother and my grandmother. What do you know, young man, about the modesty of women in the old times? In Warsaw, the murderers hanged an important woman, the wife of an elder, a saintly person. While they were dragging her to the gallows, she was afraid that her dress might rise above her knees and expose her to shame. So she put a pin into her dress, through her leg, and this was the way they hanged her."

"Were you there?"

"Others were there. My own aunt Deborah was a widow at twenty-three, and she never married again. They proposed her to a very wealthy man, but she said, 'I want to come pure to my Zorach in paradise.'"

"And you believe that she's there with him?"

"Yes, I do."

"Zorach isn't there, and she isn't there, either. Nothing remains of them but a heap of dust. She suffered in vain – this is what Morris Melnik says. In our town, there was a rich man,

Reb Zadok, a scholar. He died and left his widow a great fortune. Exactly half a year later, she married an ignorant butcher named Chazkele Scab. She'd fallen in love with him at the butcher's block."

"Well, everything's possible."

"Everything's rotten."

Morris Melnik fell silent. He lifted a teaspoon and tried to balance it on the rim of a plate. The spoon shook, tipping toward the handle end, and Morris Melnik quickly poured a little salt into the bowl of the spoon to give it equilibrium. He bit his lower lip and one of his eyes opened wide. The other he shut, as if in a wink. He seemed to have taken it as an omen that the way the spoon fell would indicate how things really stood in the world.

Reb Berish shook his head, as if in agreement with an old truth, which, although one may doubt it, still makes one despair. He lifted a tuft of his beard and studied it, as though to convince himself that it was already white. Then he said, "When a worm is buried in garbage, how can it know that there are mansions, palaces, gardens? There's a proverb: A bedbug in the wall doesn't go to a ball. You keep on babbling about the earth, but there's a heaven with stars, constellations, emanations. There are angels, seraphim, cherubim, holy chariots. In comparison with them, our little world is a piece of dust, or even less. There are some sacred sparks, but they're hidden. Even in the mud you sometimes find a diamond. Amid all this filth, there is a Baal Shem, a Rabbi Elimelech, a Berditchever, a Kotzker. Where did they come from? My own grandfather Reb Chaim was a saint. For fifty years, he fasted each Monday and Thursday. He got up every midnight to lament the destruction of the temple, in summer as well as in winter. He gave away his last penny for charity. I saw it with my own eyes."

Reb Berish began to pound his chest, which was covered with a fringed garment. His face became redder, his beard trembled.

Then he said, "You are misled, Mr. Melnik. However, a man cannot be judged in his moments of suffering. I'm going to say grace."

He took a glass, poured some water on his hands, and wiped them on the tablecloth. He began to recite aloud.

"Blessed art Thou, O Lord our God, King of the Universe, who feedest the whole world with Thy Goodness, with Grace, with Loving Kindness . . . "

In that moment, the little spoon tipped into the plate. Morris Melnik's yellow eyes filled with laughter. He rose and went to the door. He said to himself, "Well, I guess I'll go see what the women are doing."

Translated by the author

A WINDOW TO THE WORLD

Some writers begin to write with talent, quickly earn a reputation among readers and critics, and then are suddenly silenced forever. We had two such men at the Yiddish Writers' Club in Warsaw. One, Menahem Roshbom, had managed, before he was thirty, to publish three novels. The other, Zimmel Hesheles, had at the age of twenty-three written one long poem. Both got enthusiastic reviews in the Yiddish press. But then, as the saying goes, their literary wombs closed up and never opened again.

Roshbom was already in his fifties and Hesheles in his late forties when I became a member of the Writers' Club. Both were considered good chess players. I often saw them playing together. Menahem Roshbom was always humming a tune, swaying, grimacing, and trying to pluck out the remaining few hairs from his salt-and-pepper goatee. He would raise his thumb and forefinger as if to move a piece, and then pull them back as if they had been singed. It was said that he was a better player than Hesheles, but toward the end of the game he inevitably lost his patience. Menahem Roshbom was a chain-smoker. His fingers and nails were stained yellow, and he suffered from a chronic cough. It was said that he smoked even while asleep. He was tall, emaciated, wrinkled, stooped. After he stopped writing fiction, he had taken to journalism and had become the head feuilletonist at one of the two Warsaw Yiddish newspapers. Although he was sick and it was said that he was consumptive, he carried on with women, mainly actresses from the Yiddish theater. He had in his lifetime divorced three wives, and the children of all his three wives came to him for money. His steady mistress was the wife of a Yiddish actor. It was never determined why her husband allowed her to be with Roshbom. I often heard it said that Roshbom deplored being too clever, too cynical. Frequently in his conversations, and even in his articles, he belittled the value of literature and the delusions of immortality. He had never allowed himself to be honored at a banquet. If someone called him a writer, Roshbom responded:

"Maybe at one time ... "

Zimmel Hesheles was small, reserved, a lonely and silent little bachelor. His narrow face was always closely shaved and his cheeks were unusually smooth. Some thought that he was a eunuch whose beard didn't even grow. He dragged a foot and carried a cane. One of his shoes had a higher heel. His brown hair had an unmanly thickness and sheen.

For a pauper who supported himself by filling in as a proofreader during the summer vacations, Zimmel Hesheles dressed decently enough. Both summer and winter he went around in a black broad-brimmed hat, spats, and an artist's foulard. He had hardly given up his literary ambitions and let it be known that he was still writing even though he didn't publish. He belonged to the Pen Club and attended literary evenings. He exercised a professional punctiliousness. He didn't smoke, didn't hum, didn't grimace. He came each day to the Writers' Club precisely at noon, ordered a glass of tea with lemon and nothing else, read the newspapers, played a game of chess with Roshbom or someone else, and left at two when the crowd began to gather for lunch. It was said at the club that Zimmel Hesheles prepared his own meals on a hot plate and that he even did his own laundry. Someone had seen him buying cheap army bread at Kercelak Place, where bargains could be found. Zimmel Hesheles had once blurted out to the management of the journalists' association that he managed to feed and clothe himself on a sum that were he to reveal it no one would have believed him.

Menahem Roshbom was what is called an open book. But Zimmel Hesheles always sat erect over the chessboard, and after Roshbom had had his say, Zimmel would mumble: "So where does the king go?"

And we kibitzers knew that Roshbom's king had fallen into a trap. When Roshbom realized that the situation was hopeless, he would knock the chess pieces away with a sweep of his hand and say something like: "I shouldn't have moved the pawn."

And he would blow a thick cloud of smoke right into Zimmel Hesheles's face.

We younger writers often spoke of the two, probed the reasons they had stopped writing, and repeated all kinds of anecdotes and gossip, especially about Zimmel Hesheles. Was he a eunuch or simply impotent? Did he have secret relations with men? Was he really writing something or merely boasting? And what did he do with the other hours of the day and night? He was never seen at a movie, a theater, a library, or even walking. He always wore the same clothes, which looked clean and somehow as if new. Each time the young writers at the club were left without a topic of discussion, they turned to Zimmel Hesheles. Had he found the key to a perfect existence?

I felt a particular curiosity toward this individual. I constantly set programs of behavior for myself and invariably broke them. I had decided to become a vegetarian, and three days later I slipped up with a sausage. I assumed regimens of morality and spiritual hygiene, determined to devote so many hours each day to writing, reading, sleeping, exercising, and walking, but I never stuck to anything. I tried several times to start a conversation with Zimmel Hesheles, but he answered me curtly, sharply, so that soon there was nothing left to say. At times he would only shake his head or wave a hand. It was as if Zimmel Hesheles had put a lock on himself, and it appeared that he would remain so to the end of his days. Strangely enough, the book of poems he had published had vanished not only from the bookstores but from the Yiddish libraries as well. I had wanted to read it on numerous occasions, but I could not find a single copy anywhere. At that time I had already become interested in psychic research, and it occurred to me that maybe Zimmel Hesheles was what is called a spirit.

One winter evening I went to the Writers' Club instead of staying in my room and working on my never-ending novel as I had resolved. My colleagues, the young writers, came running up with particular excitement. Their eyes sparkled with that special triumph of a person who has just won a bet. One of them, Shmuel Blechman, a gossiper, said to me: "You've heard the news already?"

"What news?"

"You want to know, do you? Try to guess."

"A cow flew over the roof and laid brass eggs," I said.

"Something even more strange than that."

I mentioned a few impossibilities: The Messiah had come, Stalin had become a Zionist, the anti-Semite Nowoczynski had converted to Judaism.

Shmuel Blechman could apparently no longer bear the suspense and cried out: "Zimmel Hesheles got married!"

He clapped his hands and began to rock with laughter. The others joined in.

For some reason I wasn't in the mood to laugh, and I asked: "Who's the lucky bride?"

"Come see!"

He pushed me next door into the Large Hall, as it was called, where the older writers sat — long-standing members, not guests or beginners like us.

The walls here were tapestried and decorated with gilt-framed paintings. There was a piano and a stage where occasional lectures were held. Not far from the stage stood a table that — although anyone could sit there — was usually occupied by only the elite of the club: the president, the members of the board, editors, and the writers who were considered classicists. Foreign visitors were also entertained there, especially those from America. We beginners had given this table a name that reflected our envy: The Table of Impotents.

This time the table was filled to capacity. Seated at its head was Zimmel Hesheles, and next to him a young lady, apparently a foreigner, wearing a black hat with a broad, curving brim and a dress of a kind not seen in the Writers' Club or in the streets I frequented. Her face was girlishly narrow, her eyes large, black, and bright. I stood there agape.

One of the group pinched my neck: "Well, what do you say?"

Someone at the table barked at us to shut the door, and we went back to the smaller hall. Shmuel Blechman asked me: "So what do you say to this?"

"How do you know they're married?"

"There was an announcement in the Heint."

He rummaged among the newspapers on the table but someone had torn out the notice.

Gradually, the information began to leak out. The bride, Señorita Lena Hesheles, a relative, had come to Warsaw on a visit from Buenos Aires, fallen in love with Zimmel "at first sight," and married him. We hadn't even noticed that Zimmel Hesheles hadn't shown up at the club for a couple of days. The ceremony had taken place at a neighborhood rabbi's. Like everything else

Zimmel Hesheles did, his wedding was also intended to remain a secret. Lena Hesheles, a Spanish poetess, had brought letters of recommendation from the Argentine Pen Club to the Polish Pen Club in Warsaw, and an interview along with her photo had appeared in the Polish literary weekly. It was actually from this interview that the Yiddish Writers' Club had learned of Hesheles's marriage. The secretary of the club, himself a poet, who each summer had to wage a fresh campaign to have Hesheles hired as a substitute, had after lengthy arguments managed to persuade Hesheles to allow himself and his bride to be invited to tea.

The members of the Yiddish Writers' Club had a lot of respect for the gentile world, in which writers were connected with magazines that sold hundreds of thousands of copies. Zimmel Hesheles had opened for the Yiddish writers in Warsaw a window to the world.

For a week or two after his reception Zimmel Hesheles didn't show up at the Writers' Club. It became obvious that he was no neuter, as had been assumed, but, to the contrary, a virile man able to win the love of a young, pretty woman who wrote in Spanish. After a while, Zimmel Hesheles began coming to the Writers' Club again, no longer alone but with Lena. He no longer ordered one glass of tea but two, and cookies besides. He again played chess, and standing or sitting among the kibitzers was Lena.

Lena spoke Yiddish, but with a Spanish accent. She quickly struck up an acquaintance with us young writers, particularly the poets. As silent as Zimmel Hesheles was, so did Lena turn out to be garrulous. She talked about the Spanish writers in Argentina, the cafés, the little magazines published there, the literary feuds, intrigues, and slanders. We learned that the young writers in Argentina shared the same burden we did in Warsaw — they were kept out of the well-known magazines and found it difficult to publish a poem or story. Some of the writers published books at their own expense. The critics there displayed as little understanding of the new word and new approach in style as did the critics here. Lena had suffered particular difficulties due to her Jewishness and the fact that her parents had been Polish immigrants. She wasn't even a citizen yet, although she had been born in Argentina.

Her words evoked within us both amazement and a feeling of sympathy for a visitor who had come to us from the outside world and had married one of ours, a Yiddish poet and a pauper. When Lena expressed a desire to become better acquainted with Yiddish literature and to take lessons in Yiddish, we were all ready to serve as her tutors. Lena acquired not one teacher but several. One taught her reading, another spelling, a third explained the Hebrew words that enter into the Yiddish language. She began coming to the Writers' Club not only during the two hours her husband spent there but for long hours before and after lunch. We assumed that Zimmel Hesheles would become jealous and not let her spend time with writers her age, but he apparently trusted her. It didn't take long before a number of older writers also began to get closer to Lena. An editor of the literary section of a Yiddish newspaper had one of her poems translated, and he ran it in a Friday edition in large type, along with her photograph, which as usual came out nearly all black.

One day the inevitable happened: Lena had written a poem in Yiddish. The poem was clumsy, banal, but the young poets praised it, fell into ecstasy, and congratulated her for becoming part of Yiddish literature. They showered her with advice on how to make the poem stronger and more original, and Lena agreed to all their revisions. I assumed that Zimmel wouldn't let her publish such trash, but he seemed to be completely indifferent to her writing.

Then this happened: I had started a novella about the false messiah Jacob Frank, but by the end of the fourth chapter I hit a snag and couldn't go on. The action had expired as if on its own. I tried again and again to begin Chapter 5, but I wasted an entire notebook and nothing came of it. It was a hot summer day. I had read in Payot's The Education of the Will, or maybe in Farrell's book about spiritual hygiene, that a long walk could sometimes help overcome such an inhibition, and I decided to test this theory. I went out into the Kraków suburb and strolled along Nowy Swiat Street until it turned into Ujazdów Avenue. Along the way I stopped in front of bookstore windows. I also observed monuments, churches, and the houses where the Polish aristocracy resided. I went into ?azienki Park and lingered for a long time around the pond where swans floated. From here I could see the palace of King Poniatowski.

Young women, tall and slim in their riding habits and boots, went by on horses. They sat erect and silent in their saddles, and it seemed to me that they were privy to some secret that they concealed from others. They struck me as members of some superhuman race. It occurred to me that the angels who had fallen from heaven, the giants mentioned in the Book of Genesis, had fallen in love with such females.

Gradually I also became aware of the error I had made in my novella. Jacob Frank had been a Sephardic Jew who spoke Turkish. Yiddish had not been his mother tongue and I had no right to use a hero whose life and heritage were so alien to me. I should have stuck to only his disciples in Poland: Elisha Shur; Rabbi Nachman of Busk; and others who later converted and assumed such fancy names as Wolowski and Majewski. I was amazed that I hadn't realized this right at the very beginning.

Evening began to fall. Birds twittered. Somewhere a band was playing. Cool breezes blew from the Vistula. The sun hadn't set yet, but a full moon had already emerged prematurely. The scent of plants and flowers blended with that of fresh horse manure. Together with my literary introspection I conducted a kind of personal one as well. I had already gone through a world war and revolutions. I had lived under three regimes — the Russian, the German, and the independent Polish. Jews had been granted with the Balfour Declaration the promise of a Jewish nation. I had chucked the religion of who knows how many generations and had tried hard to believe in evolution, in a universe that had evolved from an explosion. I was barely twenty-six, but it seemed to me that I had been wandering on this planet since prehistoric times. During those twilight hours I literally sensed the immortality of souls.

Suddenly, I stopped. On a bench beneath a thickly branched tree sat Menahem Roshbom and Lena. He held her hand in his. They talked, smiled. Lena laughed. Then Roshbom leaned toward her and kissed her. I stood there for a long time dumbfounded, concealed behind a tree so that they couldn't see me. I had already read Maupassant, Strindberg, Artsybashev, Kuprin, the Polish writer Gabriela Zapolska, and a number of other authors who wrote about sex. I had even tried to translate into Yiddish Otto Weininger's Sex and Character. I myself had published stories about the unfaithfulness of husbands and wives. But this was the first time I had experienced such treachery up close. I grew ashamed of my own naïveté. My heart pounded, my throat closed, and I could barely hold back my tears. I knew full well that it was unethical to stand there spying on the lovers, but I couldn't tear myself away. Not four months had gone by since Lena had married Zimmel. He wasn't only her husband but her uncle as well.

Menahem Roshbom was maybe forty years older than she. He had a mistress or several mistresses. Had he bought her with money? Did she actually love him? Did she know what love was?

Both in the poem that had been translated into Polish and in her Yiddish one, Lena had spoken of the holiness of love. I had often heard my father say, in his disputes with my elder brother, Joshua, that those who were in love were adulterers and liars, and that the novels describing these feelings were a deadly poison. Father contended that lovers didn't love the other party but only themselves. Should the female become sick or crippled, God forbid, the lecher would leave her for another. At that time I had been too young to mix into these discussions, but secretly I had sided with my brother, who argued that arranging matches through a marriage broker was Asiatic, fanatical, an anachronism left over from the Middle Ages. At that time I had taken a holy vow to marry only for love.

It grew dark and the two figures on the bench merged into a cluster of shadows. I turned off to a side, went out another exit, and took an open streetcar home. That summer night was one of those said to drive people mad. The sun had long since set, but the sky retained the brightness of day. Waves of heat fell from it. Couples by the swarms strolled along the sidewalks. They didn't walk but seemed rather to be dancing — the men in light-colored suits and straw hats, the women in hats adorned with fruits and flowers, and dresses revealing the curves and sways of their breasts, hips, loins. They were all intoxicated by love but I gazed at them with pity. They were all wallowing up to their chins in lies and deceit. I was tired and my bones ached. Old age had come down upon me. For the first time I resented that there did not exist a Jewish cloister where those who had realized the vanity of all human efforts could hide.

That night I didn't close an eye until the light of dawn. When I fell asleep, nightmares woke me. The pillow beneath my head grew soaked. Mosquitoes buzzed about my ears and bit me. From outside I heard the cries of drunks or victims of assault. I kept on hearing my father's voice. He was preaching a long sermon to me, but what he was saying I could not grasp. I got up after eleven and although I had skipped dinner, my stomach was bloated and my tongue coated. I had a quick cup of coffee at a café and went to the Writers' Club. Maybe I would meet the protagonists of yesterday's drama there? Yes, they were all present. Zimmel Hesheles, Lena, Menahem Roshbom. Zimmel Hesheles and Menahem Roshbom played chess, and Lena sat alongside and kibitzed. I stood behind her, but she didn't notice me. Roshbom's position on the chessboard was critical. He grunted, pulled the hair of his beard, grimaced, drew the cigarette smoke deeply into his lungs. For a while it seemed that, in his great confusion, he had swallowed the smoke, but suddenly it burst forth from both his mouth and his hairy nostrils. I even imagined that whirls of smoke escaped from his beard.

Zimmel Hesheles asked: "So where goes the king?"

"Yes, where goes the king?" Lena echoed.

She cast an inquisitive and radiant glance at Roshbom, who replied: "Madam, don't fret. I have a thousand ways. I'll teach him such a lesson, he'll think twice before he pulls any more filthy stunts. I'll tear him to shreds, the bungler."

Then he waved his hand so that the pieces scattered.

"I shouldn't have moved the rook."

I left the club. On the stairs I made a vow never to come back. I kept this vow for two and a half weeks.

When I came back to the club, Shmuel Blechman asked me: "Where did you disappear to? Lena Hesheles read one of your stories and she's simply enraptured. She's been looking for you. She wants to translate it into Spanish. You lucky dog. It's for you that she's going to open a window into the world."

"She's already done it," I said.

"What do you mean?"

"He likes to play the big shot," remarked another of the young writers.

They all winked and laughed.

I didn't wait for her.

Translated by Joseph Singer

ON A SHIP

The Argentine ship *La Plata* was sailing from New York to Buenos Aires. The Theatre Solail, which had invited me to the première of my play, had sent me a first-class ticket. The trip was to take eighteen days. We were supposed to stop in Trinidad, Venezuela, and Brazil. The month of October was warm even in New York, and after a few days of sailing to the south it became hot. I sat on the deck in a lounge chair and near me another passenger sat reading the Book of Job. He was a little man with milk-white hair that hung on his neck in tufts and with the young face of a schoolboy. In his black eyes there was the doleful mildness sometimes seen in people who suffer from a chronic disease. He nodded his head as he read, and I imagined he was saying, "Yes, yes, yes, right, right, right." He wore a pink shirt, pants that hung on broad old-fashioned suspenders, and a Panama hat. He smoked a long cigar.

On the other side of the deck sat a young couple with a little girl who seemed to be the delight of all the passengers. Everyone smiled at her and tried to play with her. She was a child of about three, with yellow curls, large blue eyes, and extraordinary white and delicate skin. She looked like a doll and wore a white lace dress with folds and ribbons as dolls are sometimes outfitted. She spoke French and also a few words of English. Her name was Mimi.

For some reason, Mimi had become infatuated with my neighbor. Every few minutes she would run over to him, her little hands spread out, all joy and playfulness. She tried to get his attention by tugging at the cuff of his pants, at his sleeve, at his book. He would immediately put down the Bible, catch Mimi in his short arms, kiss her forehead, and start talking to her in a mixture of French and English – both languages in a foreign accent – with a dash of Galician Yiddish. He bounced her on his knees, shook her little hands, and held out his index finger, which she grabbed and pulled toward her. Each time, she attempted to take off his reading glasses, but he would say to her, "Darling, *sois sage*. Leave my glasses in peace. *Je lis livre*. Be a good *meidele*."

The little one laughed and tried to mimic his gibberish. He searched his pockets for something she could play with. He gave her his fountain pen to hold. He took off his wristwatch and showed her how the second hand moved. He took out a cigar and pulled off the ring of gold paper and offered it to her. For a while Mimi looked at it half with curiosity and half with mockery. Then she attacked his glasses again. Soon her mother came over and took her away. I said to him, "When you start playing with a child, it's a story without an end."

He looked at me with a kind of fatherly indulgence and replied, "If we could get half as much joy from adults as from children, this world would be a paradise. My name is Isadore Lemberger."

We began to talk and he told me that he was born in Galicia, had been living in Los Angeles for over forty years, and had recently retired and given his furniture business to his three sons-in-law. I asked him where he was going. He became thoughtful, remained silent for a while, and then said, "I'll either go directly to Argentina, or I stop over in Brazil. I don't know yet myself. The main thing is that I'm going."

"A pleasure trip?"

Chapter Twenty Three

"Hey-ho-me-daddio," she said jauntily.

Win, lose or die screaming, this was it. There was no point in worrying. Yes, she had said that not very long ago at all and was still dawdling, but now she was saying it again. Actions were meant to speak louder than words and, at that moment, their actions were mute. They were standing at the back of the class, hoping they wouldn't be picked out for the show and tell they'd neglected to bring. Their actions were staring at the floor, avoiding eye contact lest they draw attention to their inactivity.

"Come on, Billy."

Puddlebrain stepped beneath the cloak of branches. Billy went with her. It was like being suddenly immersed in water. Sounds were muffled and distant. There was a pressure on the chest and a feeling of wading against a strong current that wanted nothing more than to wash you back the way you'd come! They fought against it, digging their heels into the earth to try and gain traction.

It was hard to believe that mere trees could exert such a force. In fact, these sensations could quite easily have been simply in their heads, dread dragging them down, but it didn't matter. The result was the same. Puddlebrain and Billy were moving as if in slow motion. It would have been easier to walk through thick treacle. As they moved forward, they also seemed to be moving slower as if the treacle was getting thicker. They could hear cracks and pops from far away and could see the branches unhurriedly claw down towards them. But they *couldn't* give up! Billy was sweating from the strain and Puddlebrain was tiring quickly. She imagined herself stuck there – too tired to either go on or turn back, held forever in

"You might call it that, but what pleasure is there when one travels alone? My wife died a year and a half ago, and with her everything is gone. The passengers here are almost all Spanish. The ones who speak English are young people and not my kind. So they placed me at a table by myself. A wagon pulled by oxen could pass between one course and the next. The music plays but my mind is still not on the music. Where are you going?"

I told him about my play and invitation. He wanted to know all the details. Then he said:

"At least you travel with a purpose. I'm running away from funerals. I belong to a synagogue. I'm a Freemason. I support Palestine. I come from Tarnow and have many landsmen. I have been in business for years and know thousands of people. When I was young and had a wife and small children, I didn't realize that people were dying. That was something that happened to others, not to those around me. Now everybody is dying. I buy the morning paper, and the moment I open it I see that someone from my circle has died. Sometimes it's not one but two, three, or even five. And the illnesses! This one had a heart attack and another got cancer. I brought a large part of my family over from Galicia and everyone is sick. I'm already known in all the hospitals. I am a regular visitor to the cemetery. The large broom sweeps all of us away. There are cold-blooded people who don't care. I even know monsters who think going to a funeral is fun. They meet their cronies, they go out and get drunk – they pretend they will live forever. But I cannot deceive myself. Every time I hear bad news something in my heart is torn. Such is my nature that even if I meet a person once, he is not a stranger to me. I reached the point where I couldn't stand it anymore. I went to my doctor and he said, 'Why don't you take a trip? You don't know anyone in Buenos Aires and Rio, and you will save yourself all this pain.' Her she is again."

Isadore Lemberger took off his glasses and said, "*Mamele*, everything yes, but not my glasses. If you break my glasses, what will I read with? *Tu comprends*? *Non, non, non*."

I invited Isadore Lemberger to sit at my table. He thought it over and said:

"I thank you. It would be wonderful. You are a Yiddish writer and what better company could I desire? But as I told you, I become attached to people, and I am afraid. If we share a table all these days, we will become like brothers, and God forbid if something should happen. Please forgive me for talking nonsense. This has become an obsession. I don't want to be close to anybody. As a matter of fact, I have a relative in Montevideo and I'm not going to visit him. As long as I don't know him, he's only a name to me. Once I meet him, I will become terribly concerned. This began when my wife got sick, and since her death I worry about everyone."

We walked down to the lounge and we played chess. Between games he told me about the furniture business, about the changing population of Los Angels, about his journey to America almost fifty years before – how he traveled steerage, was kept on Ellis Island for five days, and got his first job in New York sewing buttons on pants for two dollars a week. Later, when I came to the dining room for supper, I saw him sitting alone at his table. He was still reading the Book of Job. The prophet Jonah tried to flee from God unto Tarshish, and Isadore Lemberger was fleeing from death unto Buenos Aires. The band was playing Spanish melodies and American songs. Through the window I could see the setting sun – unusually large and red. The sky had been blue and clear for days. Now, toward evening, a thick fog appeared. In the middle of the room sat the captain and his crew. They seemed to be talking about the weather because they kept on pointing to the porthole. One of them was the ship's doctor. He had given me a smallpox vaccination, since I had forgotten to get one before we embarked. He was the kind of doctor that would be called a "blacksmith" in Yiddish. He had scratched me so hard that I could barely stop myself from screaming. He was tall, with a long face and watery eyes set wide apart. His flax-colored crew-cut reminded me of a pig's bristles. The gold of his épaulettes glistened. He was cutting a half-raw steak in a plate full of blood.

After supper the passengers went to dance or to bet on "races" played with little wooden horses. I went to my cabin. Instead of a porthole it had a square window. Outside, the sky had become overcast. The waves rose, black and heavy like lava. My tie, which I had hung over the sink, began to perform gymnastic feats. It stretched out straight and stiff, it turned to the right, then to the left, and once in a while it quivered. Were we entering a hurricane? I read in bed for a while and then turned off the light. Although it was dark outside, the ocean's turbulence was reflected in the mirror. Once in a while there was a flash of lightning. I fell asleep and when I awoke it was still lightning and thundering and a heavy rain was beating down on the ocean. The ship's motors droned. My toothbrush tinkled in its glass. The glass rang in its stand. All the springs in the mattress under me were vibrating. The insides of the ship moaned as though they were about to split. The black sky rose, receding into the cosmic heights. Then it went down and collapsed like a tent. In all this racket there was an uncanny silence in the corridor, as if the other passengers had deserted their cabins and run to the lifeboats.

I kept on dozing off and awakening. I heard a whistling sound but I couldn't make out if it was outside or in my ear. In my dream the gale was both real and a story. Although the cabin was cold, my pajamas were damp with perspiration. The next morning it was as dark as dusk. I dressed and went to eat breakfast. The dining room was half empty. Isadore Lemberger was not at his table. Was he sick? I tried to go outside, but the deck was roped off. It looked as though it had been scrubbed all night. The wind slammed the door in my face. At lunchtime there were even fewer passengers in the dining room than at breakfast. The band did not play. Some of the crew members were missing from the captain's table, the doctor among them. The waiter told me in broken English that at this time of year storms were rare in this part of the Atlantic.

A few days passed. The ship had been moving unusually slowly. Its chimney bellowed like an ox. The ocean spray kept on pelting my window. I was invited to a cocktail party given by the captain. Only a few attended. I noticed that the captain and the crew members were whispering and exchanging worried looks. I went to the purser to ask the number of Isadore Lemberger's cabin. I knocked at his door and no one answered. I tried to open it, but it was locked. I became suspicious. Did something happen to Isadore Lemberger? The man looked to me not in the best of health. Yes, one gets attached quicker than one thinks, I said to myself. In my imagination Isadore Lemberger was lying on his bed with a sheet over his face – dead, a man who ran away from funerals and missed his own funeral. I once heard that those who died on a ship are thrown into the sea. Even though there was no reason for my assumption that Isadore Lemberger was dead or dangerously sick – he could have been suffering from sea sickness and nothing else – I somehow felt that something bad had happened to him. I brooded about him, his family, and about what he could be doing.

On the fifth day the rain stopped, the clouds dispersed, and the sun came out, freshly bathed and golden. The stewards put the lounge chairs back on the deck. All the sick people appeared, healthy and hardy, as if they had just been pretending. At lunchtime I saw Isadore Lemberger in the dining room. His face was yellowish and there was a gloomy look in his eyes. I greeted him and he barely answered me. I decided that he was angry with me for hot having visited him. The doctor had returned to the captain's table. He drank one glass of wine after another but for some reason he remained silent. He did not talk or laugh in his wooden voice.

Later in the day I went out on the deck with a book. Instead of lounging on the chairs and enjoying the good weather, all the passengers stood in clusters whispering. Isadore Lemberger leaned against the rail, his head low as though he were searching for something in the water.

I touched his shoulder. "Mr. Lemberger."

He started. "Yes?"

"I want to tell you that I asked the purser for the number of your cabin. I went there and no one answered. I didn't want to disturb you anymore."

Isadore Lemberger looked at me in confusion. "Thank you, but what do you say about this misfortune?"

"What misfortune?"

"You don't know, or are you just pretending?"

"I really don't know."

"Well, it's good to be a writer. They don't live here, but in the clouds."

"What happened?"

"Mimi is dead."

Isadore Lemberger did not say the words – he screamed them.

"God in heaven!"

"The doctor – that butcher, that murderer – poisoned her. She came down with a fever and he gave her an overdose of medicine that could have killed a horse, let alone such a delicate baby. He should burn like fire. He should be killed. Such callous people can make you despise humanity. How is it that everybody knows about it except for you?"

"No one told me."

"Then how come I know? You hide from the truth. A real writer doesn't go up into an ivory tower. He lives among people. Please forgive me, this was not a child but a little angel. I had hoped at least to find rest on the ship. And suddenly such a blow! The angel of death is everywhere."

He stood there, his face worn and wrinkled, unshaven, with bloodshot eyes. He said, "Of all boats, I had to choose this one. Is this an accident? An act of God? And I, idiot that I am, was afraid to give her my glasses. You may think I'm mad, but maybe that was the reason she developed a fever. That child was not of this world and to say no to her was murder. I will not forgive myself until the day I die."

For a while we were both silent. Then I said, "You torture yourself for sins you have not committed."

Isadore Lemberger drew back. He stared at me, perplexed. Then he understood. "Yes," he said, "the world belongs to those with hearts of stone. Sometimes I think that God Himself is one of them."

Translated by the author and Nancy Gerstein

ADVICE

"Is this your advice?" she asked.

"Yes, this is my advice" I replied.

"In other words, I should act just as I am."

"This is the best things any person can do."

"Well, thank you, thank you. My so-called friends advised me to do the exact opposite: to pretend, laugh, cry, talk nonsense. I don't have to tell you that I could do this easily. There's a little of the maniac in every human being."

"True, but that's precisely why you have to be careful."

"This is my opinion too. The moment one begins to play-act, where's the limit? On the other hand, if my behavior is too normal, I'm again a fraud. In America people often speak about a nervous breakdown. What is a nervous breakdown? I never know exactly what these words mean. In the old country this did not exist. If by a nervous breakdown they mean a state of intense anguish, when a person wants to jump out of his own skin or can hardly resist throwing himself from a window, then I have had not one nervous breakdown, but a thousand. There's not a day when I don't go through a catastrophe. Shakespeare's 'To be or not to be' is for me a constant actuality."

"I believe that the doctor will recognize your sickness and you will receive your rightful compensation," I said.

"How will he recognize it? I can act normal, uncannily normal. I could deceive the greatest psychiatrists. Some time ago a would-be analyst tried to make a guinea pig out of me. He told me to lie down on a sofa and talk. I decided to make a fool of him and said things that fit right in with his theories. I've read Freud, Adler, Jung, and even Wilhelm Stekel. I know all their ideas and case histories. I invented a dream with a classic example of an Oedipus complex. For good measure I added one with an Electra complex and threw in a bit of narcissism too. The young man was delighted. Then I turned everything topsy-turvy and cooked up a broth that would have stumped every single expert of the human soul.

"What I'm trying to say is this: with me everything is a game. Even being natural. So why shouldn't I pretend to be crazy, especially when it's useful to me? You must know that a Yekke will always be a Yekke, even if he's a Jew. They judge everything by appearance. They have their accepted symptoms and standards. If I answer all the doctor's questions correctly and act perfectly balanced, his verdict will be that I have nerves of steel and I'm not entitled to a penny's worth of compensation. Actually my nerves are completely shot. I won't tell it to the doctor but you may know it. There's not a single ailment in the textbook of mental illnesses from which I don't suffer.

"They categorize insanity: schizophrenia, paranoia, hysteria, and use many such words. They've put the human soul in little drawers, listing the contents on the outside. But what should one do if one has all the symptoms at the same time? Among the insane themselves there are those who are normally insane and there are those who are abnormally insane. My insanity is of the latter. I discredit all their textbooks, all their prognoses, all their wisdom. I'm so insane that I'm sane. My real tragedy is that I'm a compulsive actress. If I don't play one part, I play another. Because of this, your advice to me is invalid. I can only be true to the part I happen to be in at that time. Do you understand me?"

"Yes I do."

"Nevertheless you suggested that I be myself. This is like telling a mask or a collection of masks to become a face. How can one turn a hundred masks into one real face?"

"Well, you alone must make the decision."

The woman laughed.

"It's easy to say 'decision' and to use the word 'alone.'

"First of all, I'm not capable of making any decision. If I could decide something, my situation wouldn't be what it is. In 1945, when I was released from the concentration camp, I was young and good looking. Scores of men, hundreds of them, wanted to marry me. Many of them had lost their wives and wanted to have someone to hold onto. The ugliest women, creatures who in normal times would have been spat at, were snatched up. So you can imagine how many proposals I got. It was then that I discovered I'd completely lost the power to make up my mind. I said yes and it wasn't yes. I said no and it wasn't no. For a while I thought I was in love with someone and I was ready to become his wife. Suddenly he disgusted me. In the Displaced Persons Camp in Germany, where I stayed three years after the war while waiting for a visa to America, all the men became my enemies. They accused me of being flirty and light-minded, and upbraided me for teasing Holocaust survivors. Not only can't I make big decisions, even small ones throw me into a panic. Before coming to meet you here today, I stood in front of my closet for over three quarters of an hour, unable to choose a dress to wear. It isn't that I have so many of dresses. I only have a few. I realized that it didn't matter one bit what I wore. After all, it wasn't as though I was going to meet my future husband. I didn't have to dress to impress you. I said to myself, 'Itta Rochel, put on any dress, and don't be an idiot,' but this didn't help pull me out of my ridiculous dilemma.

"You mentioned that the decision must be made *alone,* assuming that every human being has the power to be alone.

Isolated as I am, my case is such that I'm never alone. Many people live in me. I am Itta Rochel, and my mother, peace be with her, and my aunt Freidl, and my girlfriend Stefa whom the Nazis hacked into pieces in my presence, as well as multitudes of others whom I don't know. Who are they? Why have they chosen to dwell in me? I sit down to drink a cup of coffee and find myself listening to a conversation going on in my mind. I hear arguments and heated debates. If I don't make an effort to listen, the whole thing takes place almost without my awareness – as if many records were being played inside me. I know that this comparison doesn't make things clearer, but in what other way could I describe these things to you? I hear and I don't hear. I see and I don't see. When I do pay attention, the phrases bewilder and frighten me. Some of these forced companions of mine speak Hebrew, a language I never studied, or German, which I hardly know. They use such bizarre expressions that I burst out laughing. I'm a part of a collective that I cannot identify. I have no notion of what keeps it together. Despite all this noise, I think clearly and logically. Imagine, I've become a bookkeeper here in America. Not just a girl who writes out bills. I carry the whole business in my head. I'm a bookkeeper in name only. Actually I'm the manager, cashier, buyer, seller, and everything else. My boss, a German refugee, is a sick man, and he depends entirely on me. In my own way, I'm highly successful, even though my salary is still very small. You know Europeans, how old fashioned they are, and stingy too. Can you image me being a shrewd business woman?"

"Yes, it's possible."

"I'm both terribly sober and drunk as Lot. Long ago I resigned from life and from everything it can offer. I dwell in the valley of the dead, as they say. Just the same I like to eat well and to dress well. I love music. I read all the new books even though they're trash. I seldom go anywhere, but if I do, I'm not what they call a party-pooper. And so it is with everything. I can be extremely interested while dying of boredom. I have no reason to be concerned about my health. If I was told that I had cancer, it would bother me as much as last year's snow. Still, I take great care of my health and lately I've given up smoking.

"There are moments when these contradictions drive me crazy. For example, I'm a complete atheist. A person who has seen what I've seen cannot believe in God. I will even go so far as to say that faith in God is a betrayal of the Nazi victims. Still, I often talk to Him, and even pray. Some religious grandmother of mine is reciting a prayer through me. The same is true of my Jewishness. What binds me to the Jews? Absolutely nothing. I've seen Jews drag other Jews into the gas chambers. I've seen Jews dance in night clubs while in the gutters outside other Jews were dying without a crust of bread. What are Jews? Why be a Jew when you don't believe in the Coming of the Messiah and all the rest?

"But at the same time, a Jewish fire burns in me. When I read in the newspapers that some injustice has been inflicted on a Jew in Morocco, my blood boils and I crave revenge. I cannot describe what I went through during the time of the Eichmann trial. I constantly feared that I might die before Eichmann was sentenced, or that the President of Israel might rescind his death sentence. But what is the purpose of taking up your time? As a matter of fact, I knew even before coming here that you could not give me any advice."

"It's interesting, anyway."

"Thank you. What else could you say? The real reason for my coming to you is that I find in your writings much that reminds me of myself. When I read your works I kept on asking myself: Who stole from whom? I began to suspect that you are perhaps one of my dybbuks. By the way, what time is it?"

"Ten minutes to two."

"My God, I've been sitting here for two hours. You have the patience of an angel. Are you really so good or are you playing a part?"

"Both."

"Sure. I still want to ask you one more question, then I won't bother you anymore. Tell me frankly. In your opinion, am I insane?"

"Absolutely not."

"So what am I?"

"A child of a decimated generation."

"Is that all?"

"That's enough."

"In that case reparations are not due me."

"Not according to German law."

Translated by the author and Ruth Schachner

TRIO

At a banquet organized for me by the Yiddish writers in Rio de Janeiro, three tiny people – two men and a woman – sat on the far side of a long table. I knew all the others, because they either belonged to the literary profession or were connected with Yiddish culture, but these three I had never seen before during my lectures there.

The stranger to the right was blond, with blue eyes, and a yellow mustache, which he curled like a Polish squire. His face seemed familiar to me. He glanced at me as if he were thinking: You don't recognize me, but you will soon know who I am and be surprised. He wore a sand-colored suit, a shirt of the same hue, and a tie with a pearl stick-pin in the knot. He had a short nose, sunken cheeks, and his lips kept smiling and moving. His bald spot gleamed like a mirror. He appeared to be in his fifties but could have been older. Once in a while, I had a feeling that I was about to recognize him, but the noise at the table distracted me. The other two I was certain I had never met. The woman to the left was also light-skinned with yellow hair. She wore a broad-brimmed straw hat that shadowed her round face. From a distance, she looked almost girlish, but I sensed that her youthfulness was a façade – a result of cosmetics. Her eyes were deep sunken, and I imagined I could see her wrinkles. I had the impression that she was trying her best to be inconspicuous and shrink into the seat in which she was sitting. She barely touched the food that was put before her, and kept silent throughout the meal. When the men on either side spoke to her, she just nodded.

"Is she sick?" I asked myself. "Or has she suffered some misfortune?" I didn't know why, but I kept looking at her. The few times our eyes met, she reproachfully turned away.

The little man in the middle had shoulder-length, jet black hair and a tiny beard on the tip of his chin. He wore a velvet jacket and a flowing tie. He made Hassidic grimaces as if he had just left the yeshiva. Once in a while he smiled, showing sparse blackish teeth. Even though he must have been in his late forties, he reminded me of a *heder*-boy. When they served him chicken, he tried with childish clumsiness to use his knife and fork. Then he put aside his silverware and began to tear pieces of mean and skin with his bare fingers.

As is the custom with Yiddish writers, after the dessert was served the chairman rapped on the table and announced that the orations would begin. People raised their hands to indicate that they wanted to speak. The dark little man with the long hair kept waving his hand to be recognized as a speaker, but the chairman didn't' see him – or pretended not to. After the speeches, I asked the chairman why he had ignored the little man. He smiled contemptuously and replied, "They weren't invited. They came on their own."

"Who are they?"

"It's a long story. I'll tell you later."

When the banquet was finished, the little blond man with the yellow mustache approached me and asked in a sarcastic tone, "You really don't recognize me, or you don't want to recognize me?"

"God is my witness that – "

"Halpern. Zelig Halpern."

I was abashed. I almost cried out, "Didn't you die?"

Zelig Halpern had been one of the most talented writers in Warsaw. Although he was ten years older than I was, we had been friends. Then he left Poland without farewells. Some believed he emigrated to Bolivia or Uruguay. Years passed and I never saw his name in a literary magazine. I remembered that once, years later, when I was in New York, a visiting writer from South America told me that Zelig Halpern had died. Either my informant had mistaken the name, or the whole incident had been a dream, because here Zelig Halpern stood before me. In an instant, I recognized his face and his voice. In Warsaw he was poor. He even ate for a time in a soup kitchen for intelligentsia. Later, he worked for a bookbinder. Now he looked like a dandy.

I mumbled, "Really, I didn't know that – "

"You don't need to apologize. I have, so to say, burned all my bridges. I have become a silent man, a living corpse. This is what fate decreed for me."

"You look young."

"Well, I became quite wealthy in Brazil. I have here one of the largest binderies, and other investments also. I have become what we used to call a bloodsucker – a capitalist. I am completely alienated from the literati. Is there anyone to be close to? But I still read a Yiddish book. I read everything you write. I was not invited to this affair, but I paid and I came."

He extended his hand to me – a small bony hand – and he pressed mine with such strength that I almost cried out. His blue eyes gleamed triumphantly.

"Not bad for someone my age? I became quite a sportsman in Brazil. I'm in love with the ocean and I swim all year round, summer and winter. I walk at least ten kilometers a day. And I lift weights. I do everything except what I should do – write."

"Why, Zelig, why?"

"Oh, there's so much to tell. In my life things went awry. Recently, fate played a trick on me which even I did not deserve. I found myself in a situation where I either had to make an end to everything or to swallow the most bitter pill which destiny can produce. I decided that the grave will wait. Actually, I will be cremated. We must get together. I would invite you to visit me, but I have no home. Don't look so astonished – I have a house like a palace, but it's not mine."

"You speak in riddles."

"Yes, riddles. But when we speak, there will be no riddles. Only in a sense. Actually, my whole life has become one great riddle for which there is no solution."

I wanted to ask him who the two people were with whom he sat, but others began talking to me. They shot angry glances at Zelig. We quickly agreed to meet for breakfast the next morning at nine o'clock in the café of Hotel Copacabana. I was staying at the Hotel Lancaster. Zelig Halpern again shook hands with me, but without his former show of strength. His blue eyes sparkled. He certainly did not look like a man who had experienced great tragedy.

Exactly at nine o'clock the next morning, I stood before the Hotel Copacabana. A limousine drove up and a chauffeur opened the door. Zelig Halpern stepped out of the car. He led me to a terrace that overlooked the Atlantic Ocean. We drank papaya juice, ate mangoes, and I inhaled the aroma of the Brazilian coffee and the freshness of the sea. It was autumn in New York. Here in Brazil spring was breaking through. Zelig wore a cream-colored suit and a Panama hat. He said to me, "It's hard to believe that this is the same boy who used to sit in the Writer's Club and read books. But you are the same – the same."

"What happened to you? You left and vanished like a stone in water."

"Oh, there's a reason for everything. What happened to me is begging to be written about, but I have left literature forever. In a bindery, one walks over books – and for something which you trample with your feet, you have no appetite. Besides, the young generation doesn't read Yiddish – neither here, nor in your

United States, not even in Israel. So for whom shall we write? For those in the old age homes? Or for my so-called colleagues? My doubts began already in Poland. To be a real writer, one needs a passion for literature. And this I was lacking. I wanted to experience life myself, not to describe how others live. When you met me in Warsaw, you must have been about twenty. I remember your telling me that you had to register for the army. But I was past thirty, and had been through a lot. I had been for many years in love with a woman."

"Yes, I know. She committed suicide."

"You have a good memory. I thought that no one remembers me anymore. Yes, she committed suicide, because her husband refused to divorce her. She did it in my home. She had a key. I came home, opened the door, and she was hanging from the ceiling, dressed up in her holiday clothes. After her death, I lost my desire for life, too. It was then that I left Warsaw. But I did not go abroad immediately. In our hometown I had a cousin, Dosha, who was in love with me. And when the other did what she did, I married my cousin. This is the woman who was sitting next to me yesterday."

"An attractive woman – but somehow sad."

"She has no reason to be gay. She is my first cousin, the daughter of my mother's brother. We are a family of short people. We Jews are allowed to marry first cousins, but for the Christian this is incest. And sometimes I think that in this respect they are right. We were brought up together, although I am older than she. As a matter of fact, I carried her in my arms. My Uncle Nachman was unlucky with his children. He had five, and only Dosha survived. Our home was full of little ones. I often used to go to my uncle's to eat meals. We were paupers, but Uncle Nachman was somewhat wealthy.

"I don't know if you noticed the resemblance between us. We are exactly the same height. We have the same features. We often speak the same words and think the same thoughts. We liked one another when she was just a twelve-year-old girl. But my uncle wanted a rich son-in-law, not a pauper. Besides, he and my mother had a long-standing quarrel. In addition, I always had the feeling that to marry Dosha would be like marrying a sister. I went to Warsaw and fell in love with Regina, the one who hanged herself. You will never know how great a love that was. Her husband worshipped her and he constantly threatened that he would shoot me. I'm tiny, and he was a giant of a man.

"When I returned to the village after the calamity with Regina, my Uncle Nachman was dead. My Aunt Feigel, Dosha's Mother, had passed away even earlier. Dosha had a job in the city hall, a rare thing for a Jewish girl in Poland. She had studied in Gymnasium in the city of Radom. We corresponded, and when I began to be published she became my most faithful reader. She even tried to translate my writings into Polish. She never stopped waiting for me. It may seem strange to you that a tiny creature as I should inspire such a great love, but so it was. You often write about the hidden powers – these hidden powers exist.

"After we were married, I realized how deep the similarities were between us. We were like identical twins. She opened her mouth to say something and I knew exactly what she was going to say. It happened not once, but every day, or ten times a day. I didn't have a physical desire for her. When we were together and I wanted to be stimulated, I had to think about Regina, or talk about her. She tolerated it – did she have a choice? Besides, she so identified herself with me, that she too became involved in my obsessions. This was more than tolerance. When I became infatuated with a woman, Dosha too became attracted to her, and very often she arranged for us to be together. One thing she always warned me about – not to become involved with a woman who wants to get married – in other words, one who would seek to take her place. She preached to me that the best thing for a married man is to have relations with another man's wife. It's convenient and it does't lead to complications. I used to ask, 'How about the Ten Commandments?' and she would answer that we were 'living in another time,' and all the other rationales. She herself was utterly virtuous.

"Many years passed. We never had children. Whose fault it was I don't know. Here in Brazil, Dosha learned to speak Portuguese perfectly, and she helped me in my business. Without her I wouldn't have achieved half of what I accomplished. Donna Halpern is known in all the printing shops. She often reproached me for abandoning my writing. She equipped an office for me, bought me a Yiddish typewriter, and promised to find a translator for me so that I might be published in Portuguese. But my yearning for the pen died with Regina.

"I would somehow have dragged my years to their conclusion if a client of mine, a printer, had not recommended a refugee girl to me. Fate must have sent her to Brazil for one purpose – to destroy me. She came to ask me for a job. The whole thing was crazy – how could I offer her a job when she didn't know a word of Portuguese? She had stopped here en route to Argentina, where she supposedly had relatives. After the Holocaust, the Jews in Brazil had brought over a number of refugees and helped them as much as possible. Many settled here – some even became rich. She's in Buenos Aries now. Her name is Lena. Since you are on your way to Argentina, there's a chance you may meet her, because the Jews there, especially the Yiddishists, stick together. She may come to one of your lectures. How does she look? It's hard to say. I have her photograph somewhere. She's far from a beauty. Her greatest power is in her eyes. A pair of terrible eyes which express the whole madness of the human species. She's little – even smaller than I am. She'd lived for a year or two in North America and before that for years in DP Camps in Germany. All I had to do that day was to tell her that I had no job for her and that would have ended it. Instead, I took her to lunch. My dear man, I had invited a demon."

Zelig Halpern finished his cup of coffee in one gulp.

"You ask what kind of person she was? Believe me, I don't know to this day. She was the biggest mythomaniac I have ever met. I am not exaggerating when I tell you that a true word never came from her mouth. Let's say she ate an omelet for breakfast. If I were to ask her, she'd say cheese, salami, herring – anything but an omelet. In the beginning, her lies puzzled me. I'd given her a job. I would send her on errands to buy stamps in the post office, or whatever I could invent. Each errand resulted in a catastrophe. She would spend the money and say that it was stolen. She even went to the police to report the theft. It was all made up. She 'd swear to me the most holy oaths that she would tell the truth. Immediately afterwards, she'd begin to tell me things that were complete inventions. The little that I know about her past was revealed when she forgot herself and inadvertently spoke the truth. That she was a Kapo for the Nazis, she admitted herself. How many lovers she had before me, and how many others she had while with me, I will never know. One thing is sure – she awakened in me a lust which I didn't even have when I was with Regina. In her devilish way, she loved me – the love of a she-demon. She flew into jealous rages, which had all the earmarks of insanity. Dosha sensed what was going on and we became bitterly hostile. She stopped coming to the business and withdrew from everything. She has a relative in San Paolo and she went to them.

"As for Lena, she started to demand that I divorce Dosha and marry her. No matter how many times I told her that this was impossible, my words fell on deaf ears. Dosha was to me not only a wife, but a sister, a mother, a daughter. But talking to Lena was like talking to a wall. A hundred times a day, she presented me with ultimatums. She harangued me constantly. Our being together became one long battle. Every few days a new crisis emerged. She also tried to commit suicide – not just to frighten me, but attempts which almost killed her. Those who belittle melodrama in theatre and literature don't know how melodramatic life can be. She laughed and cried. She wrote me letters in blood. Not a week passed that I didn't have to call an ambulance.

"After attacks of the wildest hysteria came nights of mad lovemaking and caresses that defied description. Why go on? She wore me out. She brought me to such a state that one evening I came home to Dosha – she had returned from San Paolo – and told her that we must divorce. I was ready to give her half my fortune – whatever she asked. Just as Lena was hysterical, Dosha was quiet and restrained. She listened to me and said 'You are not only my husband, you are my cousin, my brother, my child. You, our home, and what I do in our business, is the essence of my life. If I have to give this up, I must make an end to myself.'

"I knew well that Dosha was not one of those who did things halfway. I was in such a state that I started contemplating suicide myself. Hysteria is not just a sickness – it's a power. Dosha and I did not sleep nights. We kept talking and looking for a way out until we came to a decision – a bizarre decision, which we ourselves did not believe we were capable of carrying out. I told you earlier that I had severed myself from literature and literati. But there was one exception, a young man who wrote poetry, a grandson of Chassidic rabbis. He came to Brazil from the DP Camps in Germany where he had been since 1945. He arrived with one shirt and a valise full of poems. It turned out that he was a distant relative of ours and came right to us. He had gone through Majdanek. When he first came to us, I had no patience with him, but Dosha thought he was a genius. He wrote odes to her. We had lost our whole family and he kept on writing about our uncles and aunts, and calling them by their real names. The truth is that Dosha felt some love for him. You know what happens to women when they feel that old age is nearing. When Dosha decided to marry me, she thought she was marrying a writer, not a bookbinder. For years she made futile efforts to bring me back to literature.

Well, and here comes a relative, a martyr, a poet who speaks of God, angels, the mission of the Jews, the Kabbalah, Rabbi Nachman from Breslev, and what have you. He also lectured and gave interviews to the newspapers, not only the Yiddish ones but also the Portuguese papers. Our names were mentioned. I will tell you something: I wouldn't have been hurt too much if she'd had an affair with him. She was like a sister to me and if one loves one's sister, one wants her to be happy. Just the same, more than a kiss never passed between them. And even when he kissed her, it was always in my presence. This man fulfills himself completely in his writing. There are such creatures in our world. You saw him at the banquet yesterday – the one with the long dark hair. He sat next to Dosha. He is now her husband."

"Her husband?"

"Yes. This was our decision. It was my idea, not hers. Guilt, also, is a mighty force. I had to hypnotize both of them. He – Nahum is his name, Nahum Margolis – agreed that the three of us should remain friends."

"Well, this is the last word in modernism," I said.

"I haven't finished. When I thought that Paradise would begin for me, I entered a hell for which there is no name. In *The Rod of Punishment* it is written that there are seven hells, and each one is sixty times as hot as the previous one. When I came to Lena and brought her the good tidings that Dosha was willing to divorce, I thought that she would dance with joy. But her malevolent eyes, which had looked into the abyss, did not light up for a second. From her mouth poured out countless reproaches. Firstly, she did not like the fact that I had parted from Dosha in a peaceful way. She would have wanted us to end with curses, blows, perhaps with murder. Then she was indignant that Dosha kept the house and stayed on as a partner in the business. The truth is that without her, everything would have collapsed. Of course I had to give her the house – after all, I broke up the home, not she. The truth is that I could have taken everything from her and she wouldn't have demurred. This was not a divorce but a suicide pact.

"When Lena heard that Dosha was going to marry Nahum, she fell into a rage, as if Dosha had taken him away from her. My dear friend, it is true that I stopped writing, but I am still somewhat interested in human beings and their characters. In all this uproar, the one iota of a writer in me kept on asking, 'Could this be properly described?' It may sound ridiculous to you, but as Lena was hailing fire and brimstone, I had to admire her language – I never knew that Yiddish was so rich. She had picked up, during her wanderings, all of our dialects. She had saturated herself with the gutter language of Poland, Lithuania, Romania, Hungary, and who knows where else. It all gushed out like a stream of filth. She hissed profanities in a dozen vernaculars. When she cursed, her mouth became distorted like that of a frog, and the venom of the world spewed form it. Humiliated and crushed as I was, I thought: I wish someone could record all this.

"After the flood of rage came an outpouring of passion; and soon afterwards we stood under the wedding canopy. We had taken rooms here in this very hotel – a suite set aside for kings and presidents. But immediately, the first night, she quarreled with the waiters and the chambermaid. In a hotel like this, especially in South America, the service is exceedingly polite. Lately, I have been suffering from a kind of amnesia – I remember the incident, but the cause, if there was a cause, I completely forget. All I remember is that she brought things to such a pass, that we were asked to pack our bags in the middle of the night and get out."

"Where did you sleep?" I asked.

"We went to another hotel, and there we got a bed with bedbugs."

"You should write about it," I said.

"What for? That there should be another book in the world? We lay with the bedbugs and she pledged me the bliss of heaven. Then we went to Argentina, where I had the honor of meeting at least a dozen of her former lovers. Lovers is not the word. While they were running from Russia, those refugees lay in ditches and stables. Lena did not find it even necessary to hide all this from me. She loved to confess her sins. From Argentina, we flew to Uruguay, Chile, Peru, Bolivia, and everywhere men, with eyes like vultures, were awaiting her. I was so miserable that I tried to convince myself that I was happy. I heard of so many Bolshevik and Nazi atrocities that I became immune. So passed our honeymoon. One thing I avoided – bullfighting. Lena ran to see these sadistic shows with her former boyfriends. By nature I am jealous, but when you marry off your wife to another man, and you wed someone like Lena, what's the sense of being jealous? Really, I have to laugh."

Zelig Halpern took out a handkerchief, and he half-laughed and spat into it. He put it back into his pocket and said, "When we returned from that wretched honeymoon, everything was finished between us. I had gone through, in these four weeks, more agony than others in a lifetime. We already spoke about divorce the first night of our wedding. The force of hysteria and wickedness, which is also hysteria, consists in that it condenses time. I read somewhere that there are compressed stars, so called white dwarfs, of which a cubic inch of matter weighs thousands of tons. The same thing is even more true of time. Our four weeks encompassed the bitterness of generations. I came back old, broken, mortally exhausted.

"Back in Rio, Lena found one of the best lawyers in Brazil, and she so bewitched him that he fought for her tooth and nail. They wanted to take everything from me. I was ready to succumb, but Dosha heard about what was happening, and she took over. She too got a lawyer. She met with Lena and they had a confrontation. What Dosha told her, I never learned, but Lena became softer and somehow frightened. Her lawyer too became sick and tired of her. She had maneuvered so much, that she outwitted herself. Every criminal has an Achilles' heel. We settled for a sum and she left for Buenos Aires.

"Only when the nightmare had passed did I realize what I had done. It was a terrible awakening. I could easily have told Nahum to divorce Dosha and he wouldn't have resisted. He is a thoroughly passive person, a grandchild of saints, and somewhat of a saint himself. Besides, he had lived for years in the shadow of the gas chambers. But I couldn't make a fool of that Hitler victim. According to Jewish law, a man is not allowed to re-marry his wife if she has married another one. True, it was only a civil marriage, actually a sham marriage, but even so, I couldn't do it. Dosha said to me, "You can toy with me and my feelings, but leave Nahum in peace. I'm afraid of God." These were her words.

"I could have married a third time. There's no lack of widows and divorcees. The same people who maligned me were ready to give me their daughters. But this adventure had dealt me a stronger blow that I could bear. Every night I ran a high temperature. I suffered from dreadful headaches. My stomach, too, rebelled, and I began to suspect that I had an illness. I was living right here, in the Copacabana Hotel. Some doctors assured me that it was all nerves. Others kept taking blood from me and wanted to put me in a hospital. Since my days in Poland, I have had a fear of hospitals. There, as you know, a hospital and a poorhouse were synonymous. I was ready to die, but Dosha forgot all her grievance, and nursed me like a faithful wife. She left everything and sat with me day and night. Why go on? She took me home. She literally drove the Angel of Death away from me. The moment I breathed the familiar air, I started improving. Not only Dosha, but Nahum, too, tended to me as if he were my brother, not the husband of my former wife.

"You can imagine the uproar that this strange setup created among the Jews here. And even among the Gentiles, my clients. Tongues clacked. They made ashes and dust of us. There was talk that we all slept in one large bed. I had a cook who worked for me for almost twenty years and we considered her a part of the family. When she saw what we did, she packed her bags and left. Nahum, too, wanted to pack his manuscripts and run away. But we didn't let him. Not only Dosha, but I, too, became accustomed to him. Don't look at me so bewildered. He doesn't live with her. He doesn't need a woman. He never did. All he needs is paper and ink. This is God's truth.

I had believed that the institution of excommunication did not exist anymore. But we have been excommunicated. Not with the blowing of a rams' horns and the lighting of black candles – but de-facto. No one invites us anymore. Institutions that we supported for years are sending back our contributions. Nahum cannot publish anything. Dosha and I seriously considered liquidating our business and going somewhere else. But where to? No matter where we would settle, a situation like this would scandalize people. Also, Dosha is afraid that the strain and anxiety of running away would make me sick again. I don't want to bother you any longer with my troubles. The fact is that I still live with them. We go everywhere together – the former husband, the wife, and the present husband."

Zelig Halpern gave a short laugh. His blue eyes looked at me mockingly – then he became serious. I knew that he didn't tell me the whole story yet and I was tempted to question him, but

I decided not to. We sat in silence and watched the overcast sky, a sailboat walking on the water – a phantom in gray. Seagulls circled around it, shrieking. Zelig Halpern shook his head.

"An arrangement like this cannot last. One of us will have to go."

Translated by Blanche and Joseph Nevel

APUDZHAS CAME TO SAY GOODBYE

Sylvia Cohen sounds like an average name, but Sylvia was far from being an average person. At the age of seventeen, she resolved to dedicate her life to God's suffering creatures. It happened on the day her father, Sam, died in a car accident. Sylvia's mother, Leah, had died two years earlier in a fire caused by a short circuit. Sylvia had just graduated from high school and was about to enter Hunter College, but on the day her father died, she decided that she had had enough of civilization and its victims.

The Cohens had lived on the fourth floor of a tenement in Brownsville. The apartment included a fire escape, and a pigeon had built its nest there, brooding three eggs. Each day, the father of these eggs came to replace the mother while she flew off to seek food for herself and, later, for the newly-hatched younglings. The mother didn't have to go far, because Sylvia fed the whole family a mixture of millet and groats that she bought in a nearby pet store. Sylvia had her own three parakeets that she kept in a cage which was always left open. She also had a dog, Apudzhas, and a cat, Akota. Sam had left his only daughter an insurance policy that would bring her two hundred dollars a month.

It happened that the previous summer, before her father had died, Sylvia had spent her vacation on a farm near Woodridge and Mountaindale in the Catskill Mountains. She'd often taken long solitary walks through the region. Most of the guests at the farm spent the long summer days playing cards, which they often did late into the night. They also discussed at length the bargains one could find in the New York department stores and on the pushcarts on Orchard Street. But Sylvia had no patience either for cards or bargains. She liked the stillness of the forest and observing God's creatures, especially birds, about which she had read many books.

Once, while walking in the Catskills, Sylvia came to a farm lying several miles from Mountaindale. The farm belonged to an elderly couple, Morris and Yetta Hurwitz. Morris Hurwitz had for many years been a presser in a sweater factory in Brooklyn, but in his old age he had bought a farm. The ground was full of rocks, but the property included a number of apple trees and enough grass to pasture a cow, a goat, and a horse. Yetta Hurwitz also kept chickens, ducks, and a small garden where she grew onions, tomatoes, carrots, potatoes, and red radishes, as they use to be called in the old country. Every few days Morris Hurwitz would hitch his mare, Klacza, to a buggy and go, sometimes with his wife Yetta and sometimes without her, to Montaindale to buy what they needed and to pick up his mail – which consisted mostly of copies of a Yiddish newspaper from New York which he and wife read from beginning to end, including all the advertisements. The household also included two dogs, three cats, and two canaries. Morris Hurwitz received social security and a pension from the trade union to which he'd belonged for over forty years.

In the few hours Sylvia spent with the Hurwitzes, she fell in love with them. She had never met anyone so content with their lot as this couple. It was quite enough for them to do the farm work, read the newspaper, and listen to the radio, on which one could occasionally get Yiddish programs from New York. Morris said that he didn't spend even half the money he got from his pension and social security. They had all the clothes they needed and they required no luxuries. Morris sent generous donations to refugees from Hitler as well as to charitable institutions in New York and Israel. Only twice a year the couple spent several days in a hotel in Mountaindale – on Passover and for the period between Rosh Hashanah and Yom Kippur. In the winter, when it snowed heavily, Morris would hitch Klacza to a sleigh instead of the buggy. Neither Morris nor Klacza feared snow. In Poland, where the Hurwitzes had come from, the snow covered the towns and the roads all winter and no one shoveled it away.

Not only did Sylvia fall in love with the Hurwitzes, but the old couple also grew enamored of this earnest girl.

Morris proposed to Sylvia, "Since you like it so much here, come live with us."

"We'll adopt you as a daughter," Yetta Hurwitz added. "Our daughter, Mildred, lives in Winnipeg, and we hardly ever see her."

"What would my father say?" Sylvia had asked hen. "He wants me to study dentistry, but I haven't the slightest urge to drill people's teeth. I'd rather dedicate my life to helping God's creatures."

Now that Sylvia was an orphan, she decided to do what she'd always wanted, and called the Hurwitzes. They had an old-fashioned telephone hanging on the wall, and turned the crank to make the call. She managed to make the connection and Morris answered. His voice had changed. It sounded hoarse to Sylvia, and cracked.

Morris recognized her voice at once. When Sylvia asked about Yetta, Morris paused a moment then said, "Yetta fell and broke her hip. She just came back from the hospital in New York and she can't come to the phone."

When Sylvia told Morris that she wanted to move to the farm, Morris began to cough and sputter like someone struggling to hold back his tears.

He said, "God Himself has sent you to us!"

For the entire year-and-a-half that Yetta lay sick, Sylvia served as both housekeeper and nurse. After Yetta's death, Morris lived another two years. He'd grown so old and feeble that he even lacked the strength to go to town for supplies and o get the mail, and Sylvia did this for him. The daughter came from Winnipeg to pay her father a visit, but she had four children of her own and couldn't stay long. Before he died, Morris made a will leaving the farm and the house to Sylvia.

After Morris's death Sylvia was left all alone, but she was surrounded by so many creatures that depended on her, that she didn't feel lonely. God's creatures apparently sensed that they had a friend in Sylvia and they came to her when they were in trouble. Now a lame dog strayed to the farm, now a sick cat. Now a crow with a broken wing landed on the porch, and now a marten who had apparently fought with a porcupine and had to have the quills removed from his muzzle and nose. Sylvia had brought along a number of books dealing with the care and treatment of sick animals as well as medicines. At times, she even operated on some of the creatures, or used anesthetics to put them out. The neighborhood farmers heard that Sylvia treated animals for free and came to her instead of the veterinarian who was far away. Besides, some of the farmers in the Catskills were too poor to afford a veterinarian.

In spring, summer, and even in autumn, Sylvia had lots of company. Occasionally, guests from the hotels out for a stroll stopped by the farm for a glass of milk or a short chat. It happened that a car broke down along the road and the driver came in to phone for assistance or to get a can of water. Late one summer, Sylvia had to hire a day-laborer to help pick the apples that she later sold to stores in Mountaindale. Although Sylvia was American-born, she'd become accustomed to reading the Yiddish newspaper which contained articles seldom printed in English papers, accounts of kibbutzim in Israel, descriptions of Jewish life in various lands, as well as the novels and stories the Yiddish press printed in installments. Each time Sylvia read something she liked, she thought about Morris and Yetta. How they would have loved that article! Morris's eyes would light up whenever he read something that particularly intrigued him. He would say, "We have to thank God there are writers in the world! What flavor would life have without writers, without newspapers or magazines?"

How strange! Morris and Yetta were dead, yet Sylvia often sensed their presence. At night she dreamed of them just as she did of her own parents. Sometimes Sylvia literally felt that Morris and Yetta were nearby. Their spirits hovered within this old house where they had spent their best years. At times Sylvia even imagined that they spoke to her. Once she put a pan of milk on the stove to boil and forgot all about it. Suddenly she heard Yetta's voice cry out, "Sylvia, the milk will boil over!"

Sylvia shivered, then quickly dashed into the kitchen. Another time in the summer, when Klacza was grazing all night outside, Morris came to Sylvia in a dream and yelled into her ear, "The grass is wet, Klacza will get sick!"

Sylvia awoke, trembling. It had rained during the night and Klacza was eating a lot of wet grass, which bloated her stomach. It happens that a horse or cow dies from eating too much wet grass and Sylvia quickly led Klacza into the stable and saved her from death.

"Can it be that the spirits of the dead remain in a house and watch over the household?" Sylvia wondered. "Or did these voices come from my own subconscious?"

But what was the subconscious? What were people generally with all their troubles, their yearnings, their dreams? What was life? What was consciousness?

Sylvia had believed that animals possessed mysterious powers. Dogs, cats, and birds could read the human mind. The animals communicated among themselves through mind reading.

Sylvia had a dog on the farm named Apudzhas Junior. He was the son of Apudzhas, the dog that had once belonged to her father, Sam. One day, Apudzhas Junior disappeared. It was autumn. Sylvia went looking for him and to her distress discovered that the dog had wandered out onto the road to Mountaindale, and had been run over by a car. Someone had laid his body by the side of the road. Sylvia felt herself congeal with anguish. After a while she picked up the body of her beloved pet and brought it back to the farm. There, she dug a grave and buried him. That day, the other dogs on the farm howled, whimpered, and refused to eat. They lamented their departed friend.

It was a bitter day for Sylvia. Late that evening, she fell into bed and sank into a deep sleep. Precisely at daybreak she was awakened by a dog barking. Sylvia recognized Apudzhas's voice. "How is that possible?" she asked herself.

She opened the front door and by the light of the rising sun she saw Apudzhas Junior standing there and looking at her. His eyes seemed to say, "Yes, it's me. I've come to say goodbye."

Then his form dissolved and turned to nothing.

Such events can't be easily dismissed. For days afterwards Sylvia went around as if in a daze. One day she sat down and in her broken Yiddish she wrote a long letter to the Yiddish newspaper she read. Even as she did this, she was convinced the letter would never be printed, but two weeks later she was astonished to see her name in the paper. The editor had printed the entire letter, merely correcting the grammar.

Not long afterward, letters started coming in to Sylvia from a number of readers who had enjoyed similar experiences with dogs, cats, birds – even people. Some of these accounts astounded

Sylvia. It seemed life didn't end with the collapse of the body. There remained some force that could assume the appearance of the deceased being and come to express a final thanks or last wish.

One of these letters was from a veterinarian. His letter was the longest and most interesting of all. He wrote of a dog that not only appeared after death to say goodbye to his master, but even lay at his master's feet at night like he used to do in life. One night, when robbers broke into the house, this phantom dog attacked them and saved his master's life.

This letter led to an acquaintance which blossomed into a friendship, and eventually led to a marriage between Sylvia and the veterinarian. The farm where Sylvia had for so many years helped the creatures all by herself became an animal hospital, a reservation where God's creatures of every species could find food and security. Sylvia and her husband often said that the time was coming when people would stop eating the flesh of animals and wearing their skins, furs, and feathers. In that just world, they said, hunting will be considered not a sport but a crime.

INVENTIONS

Since moving to the country, I find myself growing sleepy by ten o'clock at night. I retire at the same time as my parakeets and the chickens in the coop. In bed, I peruse *Phantasms of the Living*, but I must soon turn off the light. A dreamless sleep – or one with dreams I can't recall – takes hold of me until two in the morning. At two, I wake up completely rested, my head buzzing with plans and possibilities. On the winter night I will describe, it came to me to write about a Communist – in fact, a Communist theoretician – who attends a leftist conference on world peace and sees a ghost. I saw it all clearly: the meeting hall, the portraits of Marx and Engels, the table covered with a green cloth, the Communist, Morris Krakower, a short, stocky man with a head of close-cropped hair and a pair of steely eyes behind thick-lensed pince-nez. The conference takes place in Warsaw in the thirties, the era of Stalinist terror and the Moscow Trials. Morris Krakower disguises his defense of Stalin in the jargon of Marxist theory, but everyone grasps his meaning. In his speech, he proclaims that only the dictatorship of the proletariat can insure peace, and, therefore, no deviation either to the right or to the left can be tolerated. World peace is in the hands of the N.K.V.D.

After the reports, the delegates congregate for a friendly glass of tea. Again, Comrade Krakower holds forth. Officially, he is one of the delegates, but in reality he is a representative of the Comintern. His goatee is reminiscent of Lenin's; his voice has a hard metallic ring. He is thoroughly grounded in Marxism and knows several languages; he has delivered lectures at the Sorbonne. Twice a year, he travels to Moscow. And, as if all this were not sufficient, he is also the son of a rich man: his father owns oil wells near Drohobycz. He doesn't have to be a paid Party functionary.

Morris Krakower is clever at conspiracy, but intrigue isn't necessary here. The press is admitted to the sessions; the police have infiltrated their spies, but Morris needn't fear arrest. Even if he were arrested, it would be no great tragedy. In prison, he could devote his time to reading. He would smuggle out manuscripts to arouse the masses. A few weeks of prison can only enhance the prestige of a Party worker.

Outdoors, there's a frost. Toward evening, snow falls. The tea drinking ends, and Morris Krakower heads for his hotel. The streets are smooth, white fields through which trolley cars glide half-empty. The shopkeepers have all lowered their window shades and are fast asleep. Above the rooftops, numberless stars glitter. If intelligent beings exist on other planets, Krakower reflects, perhaps their lives are also regulated by five-year plans. He smiles at the thought. His thick lips part, revealing large, square teeth.

A madwoman sits on the curb. Next to her is a basket full of old newspapers and rags. Withdrawn and dishevelled, her eyes shining fiercely, she converses with her demon. Somewhere nearby, a tomcat yowls. A night watchman in a fur jacket and hood is checking the shopkeepers' locks. Morris Krakower goes into his hotel, gets the key from the clerk, and takes the elevator to the fourth floor. The long corridor reminds him of a prison. He opens the door to his room and enters. The chambermaid has changed the bed linen. All he needs to do is undress. Tomorrow, the conference starts late, so Morris will be able to catch up on sleep.

He puts on new pajamas. How uncharismatic a barefoot leader in ill-fitting pajamas looks! He lies down on the bed and turns out the light on the night table. The room is dark and cool, and he falls asleep immediately.

Suddenly, he feels the blanket being pulled at his feet. He wakes up. What can it be? Is there a cat in the room? A dog? He shakes off his sleepiness and turns on the light. No, there's no one there. He must have imagined it. He turns the light out and goes to sleep, but someone starts to pull the blanket again. Morris has to pull it back or else become uncovered. "What kind of business is this?" he asks himself. He turns on the light once more. Apparently, his nerves are on edge. He is surprised, because he is in good health and well rested lately. Everything is going smoothly at the conference.

He removes the blanket and examines the sheet. He gets out of bed and checks to make sure the door is chained. He peeks into the closet. Nothing. "Well, I must have been dreaming," he concludes, although he knows it was no dream. "A hallucination?" Morris Krakower is annoyed at himself. He turns out the lights and goes back to bed. "Enough of this stupidity!"

But someone is definitely pulling the blanket again. Morris sits up in bed with such force that the mattress springs ring out. Someone, some invisible being, is pulling the blanket and pulling it with the strength of human hands. Morris doesn't move a muscle. Have I gone out of my mind? he thinks. Am I suffering from a nervous breakdown?

He releases the blanket, and the invisible presence, the power whose existence is impossible, immediately draws it toward the foot of the bed. Morris is uncovered to the knees. "What the devil is this?" he says aloud. He doesn't want to admit it, but he is frightened. He can hear his heart pounding. There must be some explanation. It can't be a ghost.

As soon as the word enters his mind, terror grips him. Maybe this is some kind of sabotage. But by whom? And how? The blanket has fallen off the bed entirely. Morris wants to turn the light on, but he can't find the switch. His feet are cold, but his head is hot. By accident he knocks the lamp off the night table. He jumps out of bed and tries to turn on the overhead light, but he bumps into a chair. He reaches the switch and turns on the light. The blanket is lying on the floor. The parchment lampshade has toppled from the lamp. Again, Morris looks in the closet, goes to the window and raises the blinds. The street is white, empty. He searches for a door leading to another room, but there isn't one. He bends down and feels around under the bed, opens the door to the corridor. No one is there. "Should I call the porter? But what can I tell him? No, I can't make a fool of myself!" he decides. He closes the door, locks it, and lets the blinds down. He replaces the blanket on the bed and sets the lampshade back on the lamp. "This is insane," he mutters.

Morris Krakower has broken out in a sweat, though the room is cold. The palms of his hands are moist. "It must be some kind of neurasthenia," he says, trying to reassure himself. He considers leaving the light on for a while, but is ashamed at his cowardice. "I must not allow myself to fall victim to such superstition!" He switches the light off and walks unsteadily back to his bed. He is no longer the same self-confident Morris Krakower, spokesman for the Comintern. He is a frightened man. Will whatever it is start pulling the blanket again?

For a while, Morris lies motionless. The blanket doesn't budge. Outside the window, he hears the muffled clanging of a trolley car. He is still in the center of a civilized city and not in a desert or at the North Pole. "It's all in my mind!" he reasons. "I must sleep!" He shuts his eyes. Immediately he senses a tug. No, it isn't just a tug but a strong yank. In a second, it has dragged the blanket down to his hips. Morris reaches out, grabs the blanket, and tries to jerk it back quickly. But he has to exert all his strength, because his nocturnal visitor is pulling powerfully in the opposite direction. The visitor is stronger, and Morris must yield. He wheezes, grunts, reviles him. The brief struggle leaves Morris covered with perspiration. "What woes have befallen me!" he says, repeating an expression his mother used. That such utter madness should happen to him, of all people! What could it be? "God in Heaven, can there really be demons? If so, then everything falls apart."

I had fallen asleep and dreamed one of those dreams which recur again and again over the years. I am in a windowless cellar. I either live there or use it as a hideout. The cellar is deep, dark, the dirt floor rutted and mounded. I am afraid, but I know that I must remain there for some time. I open a door and find myself in another small dark room with a straw bed that has no bedding. I sit down on the bed and try to talk myself out of my fear, but it only grows. I hear noises. Dark creatures, soft as cobwebs, creep about in the corridor, whispering. I must escape, but the way back is blocked. I go toward a second exit, but is it there? The corridor narrows, twists, descends. I am no longer walking but crawling, wormlike, toward an opening, but will I reach it? Wait! I've left something in the other room – a document, a manuscript – and I must go back for it. This isn't the only complication. It's extraordinary, but growths resembling antlers have sprouted on my arms. The last few seconds of the dream are thick with tortuous difficulties too bizarre and numerous to remember. The whole thing is fast becoming ludicrous, and even in my sleep I know that I must awaken from this nightmare, because the power that guides dreams never wishes to risk revealing itself. It is poking fun at its own devices. It throws in weird, incoherent words, transforming the illusion into a caricature.

I open my eyes and realize that I have to go to the bathroom. What an involved way to let a person know that he has to urinate! Afterward, I return to my bed and lie quietly, amazed at the deviousness of the sleeping brain. Can there be an explanation for all this? Is there some law governing nightmares? One thing is certain: this dream returns like a leitmotif in a symphony of madness.

After a while, I remind myself of my hero, Morris Krakower. What's happened to him? Oh, yes, his silent opponent is pulling harder, and Morris must let go. So engrossed is he in the tug-of-war that his fear is momentarily forgotten. Suddenly, the other being stops pulling the blanket, and Morris Krakower perceives a shape. He realizes that all this blanket pulling was just a way of drawing his attention to this apparition.

Not far from him, at the foot of the bed, stands Comrade Damschak, who a few years ago travelled to Soviet Russia, published several angry attacks there, in which he accused a number of writers of Trotskyism, and then vanished. The face is Damschak's, but the body is as if dissected, like the cadavers used in medical school to teach anatomy. The muscles and the blood vessels are laid bare. They glow with their own phosphorescent light. Morris Krakower is so stunned that he again forgets to be afraid. The apparition slowly fades before his astonished gaze. For a few minutes, only a membrane or a faint tracery like a network persists, no longer there but not completely gone. Soon even this tracery dissolves.

Morris Krakower lies motionless for minutes or perhaps seconds (who can measure time under such circumstances?). Then he reaches for the lamp and turns it on. Now he is past fear. He picks up the blanket, which has almost completely fallen off the bed. He knows with an inner certainty that he will now be left alone. This was Comrade Damschak's way of forcing him to look at his phantom.

But how? And why? How can this be understood? It defies scientific explanation. Like food stuck in the throat, which can't be swallowed or coughed up, it fixes a question in Morris's mind that can be neither answered nor dismissed. His brain falls still. For the first time in his memory, he is entirely without thoughts, as if his mind were suspended in a vacuum. He is cold, but he doesn't cover himself. He has one hope – that the whole thing was a dream. But something tells him that he knows the difference between dreaming and reality. He glances at the clock on the night table – it is a quarter past three. He holds the clock to his ear and listens to its inner mechanism at work. Outside, a trolley car passes by, and he can hear the scraping of the wheels. Reality still exists.

For a long time, Morris sits in his bed without an idea, without a theory – a Leninist who has just seen a ghost. Then he stretches out, covers himself, and lays his head on the pillow. He doesn't dare turn out the light, but he closes his eyes.

"Well, what does one do now?" he asks himself, and he can find no answer. He falls asleep, and when he wakes up again he knows the answer: it was all a dream. If that were not the case, he, Morris Krakower, would have to surrender everything: Communism, atheism, materialism, the Party, all his convictions and commitments. And what would he do then? Turn religious? Pray in the synagogue? There are facts that a man must disown, even to himself. There are secrets one must take to the grave.

One thing is clear: the real Damschak was not here, because his body is in Russia. What Morris saw was a mental image, which his brain had for some reason constructed. Perhaps it was because Morris and Damschak were close friends, and he hasn't yet made peace with the fact that Damschak turned traitor in Russia. It is possible for a man to dream while awake.

Morris Krakower falls asleep again. In the morning, when he raises the blinds, the sun bathes the room in light. The winter day is as bright as summer. Morris examines the blanket. He finds the marks that his fingers have left in the weave. The threads look as if they had been teased apart in places. So what does this prove? Undoubtedly, he really pulled the blanket. But the other end of the blanket reveals no sign of a struggle. The ghost has left no trace.

The short speech that is delivered by Comrade Krakower that evening lacks the logic, certainty, and smoothness of the one he gave the previous day. He stammers occasionally; he makes errors. He keeps removing the pince-nez from his nose and replacing them. The essence of his speech is that at the present time there is only one revolutionary party: the Communist Party. The main organ of the Party is the Central Committee, its secretariat. To doubt the Party is to doubt Marx, Lenin, Stalin, the ultimate triumph of the proletariat – in other words, to go over to the camp of capitalism, imperialism, fascism, religion, superstition.

Translated by Aliza Shevrin

THE GIFT OF THE MISHNAH

The outer door was constantly opening and closing; young men and women kept coming in or leaving. Naphtali's orphaned children had turned the house into a den for the wicked. Seated in a shaky armchair before a rickety table near the stove old Reb Israel Walden, wearing an oversized garment with ritual fringes and a skull cap, was drinking unsweetened tea and poring over a tractate of the *Mishnah*. This was his corner, from which no one could oust him. On a shelf to the left were Reb Israel's volumes of Holy Books, a legacy from the old days: a set of the *Five Books of Moses* with the *Light of Life* commentary, copies of the *Mishnah*, tomes of the *Generations of Jacob Joseph*, the *Beginning of Wisdom*, and several Talmudic tractates. Indeed, how much does one need? One could fulfill the obligation to study Jewish scripture merely by regularly repeating a single sentence of the Bible.

In this non-kosher house, Reb Israel partook only of bread and tea, which he brewed in his own teapot on the small gas-stove. Occasionally, Basheleh, his granddaughter, would buy him herring and an onion or a radish. On the Sabbath and other festival days, the old man attended services at the Sochatchover Study House whose beadle, Reb Wolf, would then invite him to his home as a guest.

Now and then, Reb Israel would raise his bushy eyebrows and stare at the rest of the household, although he was aware that such peering was a sin, for it is forbidden to gaze upon the countenance of the sinners. However, he was afflicted with cataracts, and his vision was blurred. A mist seemed to envelope the sofa, the table, the clothes closet, the bareheaded good-for-nothing boys, the girls smoking with utter shamelessness. They laughed, smoked, recited poetry, played cards – activities intended as a cover, in case of a raid by the police. Their actual interest was in holding political sessions that took care of all the world's ills. Reb Israel would catch snatches of their discussion: *regional committee, central committee, rightists, leftists, Trotskyites, functionaries, comintern.* He could not quite make out all these terms, but their intent was all too evident: to overthrow the government, launch here in Poland the same insurrection as had already taken place in Russia, shut down the Study Houses, ban commerce, hold kangaroo courts for merchants and manufacturers, and jail the rabbis. And who were the leaders of these rebels? None other than Reb Israel's own grandchildren: Basheleh, named after her virtuous grandmother Basya Kaila, and Asher Hayim, named after the Rabbi of Josefow.

Bleary-eyed, Reb Israel looked wonderingly at the cavorting snowflakes outside – the flurries, now descending, now rising, as though on second thought anxious to return to their origin. The roof across the street had turned white. The balconies were adorned with cushions of down. The swirling snow reminded the old man of long-forgotten pilgrimages to the Rabbi of Kotsk: sleighs, inns, impassable snowdrifts, snowbound huts. Although the Hanukkah festival was still far off, Reb Israel's nostrils were assailed by the odors of oil burning in a lamp, of charred wick. He heard a sacred melody within him. He ran his fingers over his furrowed forehead as he tried to recall when the lighting of the first Hanukah candle was due, and stroked his beard which had once been white but was now turning as yellow as his parchment-like face. "All is well," Reb Israel mused. "As long as man has free will, God must hide His Face." And with that he resumed his study of the tractate *Yoma*:

> Then it was the turn of the high priest to read. If he was minded to read in the linen garments he could do so; otherwise he would read in his own white vestment. The cantor of the synagogue would take a Scroll of the Law and place it in the hands of the chief of the synagogue; and the chief of the synagogue handed it to the prefect; and the prefect gave it to the high priest; and the high priest received it standing and read it standing. And he would recite 'After the death' and 'Howbeit on the tenth day'...

Next, Reb Israel glanced into the commentary of *Obadiah* of Bertinoro, and the supplementary comments of *Yom Tov*. The script was too minute and he resorted to a magnifying glass. Although he had celebrated his completion of the reading of the Mishnah more than once, each time that he read it again, he seemed to savor it afresh, as the ancient Israelites did upon finding Manna of the desert. He always stumbled upon some abstruse point which he had somehow not noticed before. Now, with total blindness – God forbid – about to befall him, he particularly relished every word, mulling it over. The words of the sages thus became indelibly impressed upon his mind. After all, what else but the Mishnah did he possess now? Once wealthy enough, Reb Israel Walden had lost all his earthly possessions during the World War. He had reared an only son, Naphtali, and typhus had claimed him. His daughter, Baila Tzirel, had immigrated to America and had never been heard from since. His wife Hannah Dvorah had died under the knife of a surgeon. Reb Israel had drained the cup of misery to the dregs. His business had crumbled, his money had turned to paper, his household effects and his clothes had deteriorated, his health had declined rapidly. Everything had turned into nothing – everything save the Torah, charity, and prayer. Since his old age now seemed to be like one long night, he would at least memorize the Mishnah.

Dusk was setting in. The frost-patterned window-panes reflected the twilight. The young men and women moved about like shadows, their lit cigarettes glowing in the dark like fiery signals. Reb Israel was overcome by lassitude. He struggled against sinking to the depths from which there might be no return, came to with a start, and found that the lamp had been lit. He tried to resume his studies, but in the dim illumination, the words of the tractate were blurred. Reb Israel kept an oil lamp handy, but his granddaughter had forgotten to refill its oil and to clean the sooty chimney. This had not been – God forbid – intentional on her part. She was simply absorbed in her dreams of the Revolution. Like bees around honey, the young fellows hovered about his short, stocky granddaughter with her beaming face and cropped hair. This way she could dominate her admirers, and preach to them, exhorting them to rally to the cause. His grandchildren were astute, Reb Israel reflected, there was no denying that fact. It was too bad that, instead of dedicating themselves to the study of Jewish scripture, they wasted their time on such affairs.

The old man grimaced as though in distress, his chin touching the tractate before him. He closed one eye. The white of the other was crisscrossed with red veins, and the pupil distended. Reb Israel delighted in the Mishnah. Talmudic study seemed to revive him as smelling salts would on a fast day, when a famished person becomes queasy and faint.

"What does an ignoramus do in his old age," he had often asked himself. Now he went on reading, "The High Priest ministers in eight pieces of raiment, and a common priest in four – in tunic, in drawers, in turban, and in sash. To these the high priest adds the breastplate, the apron, the upper garment, and the frontlet. In these he consults the Urim and Thumin"... *Will I remember all this when, God forbid, I'll be deprived of vision altogether?* he wondered.

A vision of the Holy Land now flitted across his mind. He envisioned the Temple, the court, the altar, the chambers, the sheep and oxen, the acolytes. He was unsure whether all these were a figment of his imagination or if he had seen them in a dream. He visualized knolls, edifices, narrow streets, flat roofs, pillars of dust, a setting sun. Oxen bellowed, sheep bleated. As a barefooted, long-haired prophet passed by, he was approached by young women wearing shawls, armbands, clasps and buckles. But now everything was desolate. Foxes roamed over the chalk stone earth. The sages, in their white gabardines, had retreated to caves, where they were being tried in the crucible, sustaining themselves on bread and water, or on a measure of carobs, as Reb Hanina ben Dosia had done. He, Reb Israel, had always yearned to go to Palestine and see those caves. His wife, Hannah Dvorah, may she rest in peace, used to promise him that in their old age they would bequeath all their goods to Naphtali, and then spend their last few years in the Holy Land, near the Wailing Wall, the cave of Machpelah, and the tomb of Rachel. However, man proposes, and God disposes: now he had neither the money nor the strength for such a trip. And what was more, all the scoundrels seemed to be flocking to the Holy Land now. Plucking at this white ritual locks, Reb Israel mused that wherever holiness resided, there the Evil One also lurked seeking to gain a foothold attempting to violate the queen in the very palace of the king. The mere fact that alien forces were now heading for the Holy Land indicated that the end was near. The Messiah might well be on the way. In that case, we should be spared the need of dying.

The graybeard smiled. He feared death – he had caught himself in the act. But what was fear? He recalled a proverb of which his wife had been fond: "I'm not a calf – I have no fear of slaughter."

Reb Israel awakened. Basheleh, flushed with excitement, grinning sarcastically and clutching pencil and paper, had begun to harangue the assembled group. Reb Israel noted her resemblance to Naphtali in her expression, her mannerisms, even her voice. The old man's curiosity was at last aroused. He was determined, once and for all, to ascertain what they were bickering about day and night, without getting anywhere. If only she wouldn't utter those enigmatic foreign words!

"Fellow-workers, comrades," Basheleh said, "things can't go on this way much longer. Divisions among us only play into the hands of the enemies of the working class. The opposition in our ranks is simply the work of a counter-revolutionary group, pretending to make common cause with some of the would-be revolutionaries – which are all nothing but Social-Fascists. Our enemies are delighted by their actions. As they say: one mangy sheep ruins a whole flock. Unless these opposition groups are disciplined in time, they will corrupt and demoralize us all, they'll drag the entire party into the Fascist morass."

"Comrade Walden, speak concretely, what are you aiming at?" a voice challenged. "Comrade Kleinmintz, no interruptions, if you please."

"What is she saying?" the baffled Reb Israel asked himself. "Where did she acquire all this knowledge?" As to Asher Hayim, he bore little resemblance to his sister. He had a swarthy complexion, curly hair, thick lips, a flat nose, and small roving calculating eyes. He was clowning, mimicking now one comrade, now another, and kept away from his grandfather. Reb Israel recognized in him certain idiosyncrasies that could be traced to his daughter-in-law's Hasidic family, to Reb Gershon Henich's down-to-earth tribe from Radzin. Heredity played an important part,

Reb Israel reflected. And he regretted having steered Naphtali into this marriage. Reb Gershon had been too astute.

The Hasidic dynasty of Radzin accepted only weeds, only noxious plants from the dynasty of Kotsk. Asher Hayim was their fruit: unripe, sour. The young fellow was chatting with a girl, pulling her hair mischievously from time to time. Disgusted by the sight, Reb Israel wanted to cry out "Villain! Reprobate!" But the words stuck in his throat somehow. On second thought, he was not likely to be able to change their ways.

As Reb Israel tried to resume his studies, something strange happened: he became dizzy, total darkness descended upon him, and he felt an excruciating pain in his forehead and at the tip of his nose. He struggled to hold on to his seat. "Is this the end? Am I about to die without even reciting the final prayer?" he thought in alarm. He still hoped that his spell would subside, as had been the case some years ago. But the darkness persisted. He felt a pressure in his eye, and an intense pain at his temples. Reb Israel was panic- stricken, then resigned. This looked like the 'final summons.' Job's phrase, "For the thing which I did fear has come upon me," flitted through his bewildered mind. He was tempted to scream for help, to call for a doctor. But what could a doctor do now? He recalled that Professor Pinnes had admonished him some years back that he was living on borrowed time.

Reb Israel tried to pierce the total eclipse, and he seemed to glimpse a kaleidoscope of winding lengths of cloth, swirling in variegated fiery colors; a dance macabre of sparks, flowers, stars, swooping down like locusts. Basheleh was still haranguing the group, but he could hardly hear her. A wall seemed to loom between him and the others. He touched his cold glass of tea with the tips of his fingers. Surprisingly, he felt ashamed of his misfortune before the youthful gathering. He was averse to being surrounded with questions and sardonic compassion. He recalled the Talmudic precept: "It is incumbent on a man to pronounce a benediction over the evil things that befall him, even as he gives blessing over the good." But what sort of a benediction did one pronounce on becoming blind?

Five minutes had hardly elapsed, yet Reb Israel was already becoming reconciled to his inescapable predicament. He was only annoyed at not being able to pore over any Talmudic tractates now. He would have to draw upon his memory. "He who exerts himself before the Sabbath will have food to eat on the Sabbath." Perhaps, he thought, he might regain his vision to some extent, but that was unlikely. This misfortune had hung over him for quite some time, and now he had exhausted the last glimmer of light. Now he was stone-blind.

With a mounting internal discomfort and a profusion of saliva in his mouth, as if on the verge of fainting, he had to make his way towards the kitchen to lie down for a while. He stood up, careful not to turn over the stool, the oil lamp or the teapot. He kissed the Talmudic tome, closed it as one does the doors of the Holy Ark, and in his blind state, took leave of the Mishnah. He groped his way through the cool corridor, smelling of kerosene and dirty clothes. Upon reaching the kitchen with its smell of chicory and mold, he was about to stretch out on his iron cot, when his ears were assailed by giggling. He felt someone jump up from the cot and brush against him with lascivious laughter. One of the couples had evidently been making love on his bed.

This added insult to injury. He was about to scream, but his vocal chords seemed paralyzed. Had things come to such a pass? Naphtali's home converted into a brothel – and his own bed defiled! He was trembling like an aspen leaf and his knees buckled. "Father in heaven, why do I deserve this? My sin is greater than I can bear," he mumbled.

He slumped helplessly on his cot. "Well, defilement is defilement," he reflected, after a few moment's rest. "I no longer have any free will or choice."

He lay on the straw pallet, deep in misery, aching all over, gradually yielding to despair: "Let the end come! Let everything be over with!"

As he dozed off, his pain abated, a warmth suffused his being and he had a strange dream – a place which seemed to be devoid of words and action. All he felt was a yearning not to awaken. He had become oblivious to everything, yet that forgetfulness held a peculiar meaning and bliss. He was reposing in a garden burgeoning with flowers and echoing with the symphony of twittering birds – a sort of blending of Kotsk and the Holy Land. The sage Reb Mendele seemed to be alive. The Study House resembled a hut made of boughs, thatched with reeds and adorned with grapes and lanterns. Candles were burning. The rabbi did not merely expound the Torah, but interpreted it so that words which heretofore had been abstruse were now rendered intelligible and inspiring. It must have been the realm of Eden – or the hereafter. The expounding of the Torah was like food and drink. Was that the *yain ha'meshumar* – the wine preserved in its grapes for the righteous in the world to come? And where was the Leviathan? All the enigmas had been solved. All the dead resurrected. He was once again in the company of Hannah Dvorah, Naphtali, his parents and grandparents.

"And simpleton that I am, I was haunted by fear through a lifetime," he berated himself. He was offered on a tray something akin to the gift which is handed to the priest when a firstborn is redeemed. But at this point someone nudged his elbow, as an angel nudges the child just as it is about to emerge from its mother's belly. Reb Israel came to with a start, lying bemused, gratified by his recent heavenly food. He caught the fragrance of cloves and marchpane. Staring into the darkness, he wondered if it was summer or winter. When had he gone to bed? One moment he thought he had slept seventy years, like Honi the Circle-maker, and the next that he was already in his grave. Then it dawned on him that he had gone stone-blind, that he could not distinguish any light whatsoever.

"So that's it, this seems to be it, the last temptation," he said to himself. He regretted the interruption of his dream, but comforted himself with the thought that there was something he had to attend to. It was the Mishnah, of course, he was curious to test his memory. He at once began murmuring the opening sentence of the Talmud, from what time may one recite the *Shema* in the evening, and onward, paragraph after paragraph, chapter after chapter. He had already, of course, read through the tractate Berachoth and had gone over the difficult passages of the tractate dealing with the corner of the field which must be left untouched for gleaning by the poor. Now his retentive memory opened up all these treasures again. The Mishnah seemed well preserved, hermetically sealed in his mind. He proceeded smoothly, without faltering, and reflected that the characterization of "a limed pot which loses not a drop," once made concerning Rabbi Eliezer ben Hyrkanos, might be applied to himself as well.

Judging by the prevailing quiet, the young people must have left. It occurred to Reb Israel then that he had not recited the evening prayer yet. He groped his way to the sink and made his ablutions, the cold water refreshing him somewhat. He became aware of a new faculty, a subconscious perception for which no eyes were required. Swaying back and forth, he articulated the words solemnly:

"O though that dwellest in the covert of the Most High, and abidest in the shadow of the Almighty, I will say of the Lord, Who is my refuge and my fortress, my God in whom I trust ... "

Praised be the Lord. Reb Israel prepared himself for the test. He recited the Shema of Rabbi Isaac Surin, confessed his transgressions and beat his breast. Now, deprived of sight, he found himself face to face with the Lord of the Universe. From now on there would be no distractions. The Mishnah was the treasury of delights in this world, yet remained without diminution for the world-to-come – a vineyard of the Holy Land which no Titus could ever destroy, nor any apostate violate. He was seized by pity for his grandchildren. Alas, what did they know or understand? They had been orphaned at an early age and he, their grandfather, had not paid them enough attention. His intentions had been good. He had tried to help the needy. But one cannot force one's way into Heaven. Having caused suffering and grief, one must become reconciled to it. Affliction itself gave forth compassion.

Reb Israel undressed impatiently, anxious to lie down and return to the Mishnah, his sole possession and reward.

Translated by Moshe Spiegel

THE FINAL GIFT

The very same day I moved into the small condominium apartment in Bal Harbour, I was told about my neighbor, Priscilla Levy Clark, who was a millionairess of eighty-plus, four times widowed and three times divorced. She occupied two front apartments and employed two maids and a nurse, one of whose duties it was to walk Priscilla's little dog, Snooky, a poodle. Although it seldom gets cold in that climate, Snooky had her own chinchilla coat and alligator booties. Her gold collar was studded with pearls.

Months passed without my meeting my wealthy neighbor; she suffered from arthritis and seldom left the house. But one day she invited me to visit her. It seemed she had read one of my stories in a magazine. I took exactly two steps to my left and a black maid already held the door open for me in anticipation.

I was received by an elderly woman—small, thin, with a semibald scalp dyed orange and a wizened face that was a hodgepodge of rouge, powder and mascara. She wore a gold-embroidered kimono and over scrawny wrists, bracelets hung with many jingling, jangling charms. Priscilla Levy Clark spoke in a thin, aged voice and a Southern accent. She extended a bony little hand, and I scratched my fingers on her pointed nails and elaborate rings. She told me to sit next to her so that she could hear me better with her hearing aid, and said, "Your writing evoked something in me I assumed was already lost forever. My eyes are such that, unfortunately, I can no longer read myself, but my good Mary Ann is my reader. She is herself a lover of literature. You see, she's waiting impatiently to tell you how strong her – "

After Mary Ann had paid me her quota of compliments, she went to fetch liqueur and cookies. The living room was over-furnished with pieces that were all antique; the walls densely covered with old paintings; the floor carpeted with two layers of Oriental rugs. Although the air conditioner was working, the moldy aroma of age permeated the apartment. Priscilla said, "I see that you come from Russia or Poland. My people came here from Germany some hundred years ago. My great-grandfather, David Levy, didn't go out peddling with a pack on his shoulders like the other immigrants. He was a saddlemaker by trade and he settled not in New York or Philadelphia, but in New Orleans. During the Civil War, he enlisted in the Confederate Army and worked himself up to the rank of officer, no small feat for a Jew. He became wealthy and he was elected president of a synagogue. A great part of our family later converted, but I've remained a Jew, although I'm not really religious. My maternal grandmother came from Frankfurt, and from her I heard stories similar to those you write about … "

She wouldn't let me leave until she had shown me her treasures. In some of the rooms, objects lay in piles nearly to the ceiling. She told me that what I saw was just part of her possessions. She had two more houses—one in Atlanta, and the other in New Orleans—both filled with rare objects, as well as a Park Avenue apartment in New York City, where she spent no more than two weeks out of the year. In the past two years, she hadn't been to New York at all.

She said, "I'm ashamed to say it, but such is my luck—or maybe it's a character fault—that I've been married seven times and four of my husbands left me money in addition to what I inherited from my parents, various aunts, and a cousin. I am at an age now when you can't enjoy much, but the passion for acquisition still isn't extinguished within me. When I see a rare object, something inside me lurches. I tell myself often that this is senseless, vanity of vanities, but so long as the heart keeps beating—regardless if it's with the help of pills and injections—and so long as the eyes see—be it through a mist—one isn't dead. In years gone by, I kept on writing wills then adding codicils, but I've become convinced that once you lie in the grave, others do with your estate just as they please, not according to any instructions put down on paper. The result is that I've neglected everything. I no longer know what I possess, nor do I care to know. I have one daughter in California and forty years already she's been warring with me because I allegedly wronged her father. She herself is already in her sixties and a widow. They steal from me and I can't do anything about it. Tomorrow, a fire or a flood can come. All I do is seek means to prolong death another year or two. I envy the writers. That which they create remains—if it has any value."

"Not necessarily."

"Well, there are no guarantees. May I ask you something?"

"Yes, by all means."

"Are you religious? From what I have read of you, it's hard to determine."

"Yes, but not in the accepted sense."

"You don't belong to a synagogue?"

"No."

"Of what then does your religion consist?"

"Oh, I don't believe the universe is a physical or chemical accident. Neither do I believe that the universe is blind or dead."

"So everything lives?"

"Everything there is – yes."

"What kind of solace can you find in such conviction?"

"None at all."

"Well, it was an honor and a pleasure. I'd offer you some kind of gift if I knew you were interested in nice things."

"Truly, Madam, I have too many possessions already. I've gathered so many books, letters, even manuscripts, that I no longer have any room left in my small apartment."

"Well, the day has come when everyone has too much of everything, even paupers. Even the thieves have become choosy. They take cash in large denominations only, no small change. But when I come across something interesting or unique, an urge comes over me. They've probably fabricated all kinds of slanders against me in the building, but I can't sit around with those yentas and chatter about nothing. The day people and objects cease being interesting to me, I'll call the mortician to come fetch me."

Although I lived just a door away from Priscilla Levy Clark, weeks and months went by without my seeing her. But I frequently met her servants in the corridor or the elevator. Snooky had declined to walk and the nurse was forced to carry her. Quite often, the doorman brought packages, boxes, whole crates next door. Mary Ann told me that in the past, Priscilla attended exhibitions and auctions, but lately she bought everything from catalogs.

As I did every year at the beginning of April, I left my apartment in care of the superintendent and went back to New York. I could have leased it, as others did, to the South Americans who came to Florida summers to "cool off," but this apartment represented my sole luxury and I didn't want any strangers in it. I was supposed to be back in November, but just at that time I had to take a trip to Europe and Israel, and I first came back in January.

In the limousine taking me from the airport to Bal Harbour, I met a neighbor of mine from the condominium, a landsmann from Warsaw, Mr. Sam Prager, who told me some bad news. Several men and women from the building had died; others were in the hospital. Abruptly, he asked, "You've heard what happened to Priscilla?"

"No. What?"

"Oh, it's funny. Tragic too. Actually, unbelievable. Soon after you left, a masseur came to her, a huge fellow, over six feet. Supposedly, he had been sent by her doctor who was treating her for her arthritis. Suddenly, news got around that Priscilla was about to marry him. For the women who are left in the summers without a bit of gossip since all those who move in are Spanish, this was a godsend. She, a woman in her eighties, and he, a giant, a swimmer, a drinker, a gentile. She had, apparently, grown completely senile. Before, she never went to the beach or even to the swimming pool; all of a sudden she shows up with this fellow and in a bikini yet! I wasn't there, but I was told this. The women didn't know whether to laugh or cry. Everyone promptly gathered that she had fallen prey to a gangster and they wanted to warn her, but someone let it drop that he was liable to have connections with the Mafia, and no one wants anything to do with them. Priscilla had a lawyer in Miami and she never did anything without consulting him, but it just so happened that he was in Europe. Why drag it out? The fellow took her for everything she had. He placed papers before her and she signed them. She signed everything. He supposedly arranged for an exhibition of her antiques. Trucks came and hauled everything away to this "exhibition." They literally cleaned out both her apartments. He fired her maids and the nurse ran away on her own. He sold—or tried to sell—her apartments, I'm not sure which. After he had stripped her of everything, he disappeared. He even took her last piece of jewelry. I don't know if a swindle of such proportions had ever been perpetrated before. The police are looking for him now, but speculation is that he is somewhere in Brazil, or the devil knows where. He couldn't have done all this by himself. He had to have a gang to help him. When Priscilla's lawyer came back and heard what she'd done, he made a big stink. The newspapers had themselves a field day. In the meantime, her dog had died and the old woman fell terribly sick and had to be taken to the hospital. They didn't keep her there long. Young people drop like flies, but that old wreck went through everything and survived."

"What is she doing?"

"What can she do? She suffers. When she finally caught on that she'd been taken for a ride, she alerted her daughter in California. An old woman arrived, a replica of her mother. Whoever hasn't seen these two together, doesn't know what tricks life can conjure up. When she heard that the mother had wanted to marry this racketeer, she spat in her face and went back where she came from."

"It seems Priscilla has houses in other cities."

"Speculation is that she already has nothing. The fellow transacted everything all legal and proper. Here we are, home already."

The limousine stopped and we got out. In the elevator, Prager managed to say, "Man is only the bit of marrow. When that goes bad, you might as well bury yourself alive."

During the time I'd been away, the superintendent had stacked in my foyer many books, magazines, and letters that were sent to my Florida address. Evening fell, but I didn't turn on the lights. I was too tired from the trip even to glance through my mail. I'd flown from Israel to Los Angeles, where I had a lecture date, and from there, had gone directly to Miami to avoid New York and the bother of lectures, visits, meetings with my publisher and editors. I had resolved to rest a minimum of two weeks in Bal Habour. The moment I entered my apartment with my baggage, I lay down on the sofa to take a nap. I didn't even remove my shoes.

I dozed off and was awakened by the ringing of the doorbell. Night had fallen. I went to open the door and nearly tripped over my valises. In the doorway stood Priscilla. I wouldn't have recognized her if I hadn't heard what had happened to her. She appeared even smaller than she had been. Her hair had almost all fallen out so that several white strands dangled from her otherwise naked scalp. In the light of the hallway lamp, the wizened face was as yellow as a corpse's. She wore a wrinkled rose and scuffed slippers. She said, "Don't be alarmed. This isn't a ghost you see but your neighbor, Priscilla ... "

"Come in, come in."

I took her arm, led her to a chair, and helped her sit. I turned on the lights. For a long while she sat there resting, then she commenced speaking in her needy, melancholy voice, "Pardon me for disturbing you. The super's wife told me you were back. Perhaps you've heard what's happened with me?"

"Yes, something."

"I'm already on the verge of death. I wanted to see you before I went off into eternity, and when she told me that you were back, I didn't want to wait until morning and – "

"Don't talk this way. God will help you yet."

"No. Even if there is a God, I haven't earned His help. I came because I owe you a gift."

"A gift? You owe me nothing."

"Yes. When you visited me that first time—when was it? Nearly a year already—I wanted to give you a gift. At that time I still had a lot to give. What has happened to me is like in the Book of Job: a whirlwind came and blew everything away. I read this book once as a young girl. Before you went back to New York, you made me a gift of some of your works, and when they took me to the hospital, I took them along and I resolved that if I ever saw you again, I must give you a gift in return."

"Really, you don't have to give me anything. Look how jammed my apartment is already."

"That which I want to give you—or what I can give you—won't make your apartment any more crowded. In a sense, this is an unaesthetic gift; actually, unworthy of your stature. I thought about it a long time. But it only seems so if you don't know the story behind this gift. When you know all the facts, you'll look at it entirely differently. You obviously know already that I have a flawed nature, cursed blood. I wouldn't have come to such an end if I hadn't suffered from this kind of intoxication. It may have something to do with the chemistry of my body. I've tried psycho-analysis and other therapies, but nothing has helped. I had one hope: that old age would somehow cool me, but I reached seventy, then eighty, and still these illusions didn't fade. There remained one way out: death.

"I'll make it short. My third husband, Leslie Aberdam, blessed me with the highest, most exalted love I have ever known in my life. Unfortunately, he died young. Had he lived, I might have been spared some of the inanities—you might call them crimes—I later committed against others and against myself. Most of all, I disgraced my parents. Leslie was the son of a millionaire. He was wealthy on his own account, and he showered me with presents. It was enough for me merely to mention that something appealed to me, and he promptly went out and got it for me. We often had arguments about these extravagances. I liked jewelry and all kinds of nice things, but I didn't want him to go suddenly broke and create a situation in which his father would disinherit him. A great inheritance awaited us. Leslie liked to fantasize about treasures and all the things he would buy me when he became as rich as John Rockefeller or the Aga Khan—the father, that is. All these empty fantasies became like a sickness with him. One time he asked me: 'What would you want if I suddenly got a billion dollars?' I happened to be in a silly mood and I said: 'A toilet seat made of jade.' I promptly forgot my answer. After all, the things a young couple prattles to each other! ... A few months went by. One day, a big package arrived for me from London and when I opened it, to my surprise and dismay I found a toilet seat made of jade. I don't know till this day how much this thing cost him—how many thousands of dollars or maybe even pounds. Instead of this magnanimous gesture bringing me joy, pride, the quiver of gratitude Leslie had anticipated, it evoked my contempt and I uttered words I will regret to my last breath, which is already near."

"May I ask what it was you said to him?"

"What does it matter? I told him he had the soul of a slave."

"Aha."

"This wounded him terribly and we stayed angry a long time. Later, we made up, but the wound never healed. His business started going downhill. I'm convinced that his sickness commenced from that time. Words can kill. I learned this too late. I was superficial and contrary. I didn't appreciate my great love and I never used this ridiculous gift. I wanted to forget it, and I actually did. Many, many years after his death, when I moved in here with my last husband, it occurred to me to install Leslie's gift in my bathroom, but it didn't fit and I put it away in a dresser drawer and promptly forgot it again. When the punishment I had coming to me finally descended upon me and that devil, or Angel of Death, took everything from me—literally stripped the shirt off my back—I found Leslie's gift in the drawer where I had left it. After all, who could ever have imagined that a dusty toilet seat could be worth something? My dear friend, I want to leave you this gift that was given me as an expression of the most exalted love, and which may be all that is left me of all my illusions. It occurred to me to possibly take it along with me to my grave as a token of his deep admiration, but imagine the scandal such a desecration of death would cause! It would simply transform my funeral into a farce. Oh, I have to laugh—"

Priscilla erupted in a thin, lachrymose laugh. One of her eyes shed tears while the other glowed as a kind of remnant of her youthful mockery at Leslie's devotion and her own falseness, and at the whole institution called love. In that same moment, I perceived the kind of person she had once been and the source of the unholy power she had possessed.

I began to object that I couldn't accept this present and suggested that if she had been left without means, she might possibly sell it somewhere, but at that moment the telephone rang simultaneously in my kitchen and my bedroom. For a moment, I deliberated as to which room to answer the call in, and presently, I dashed toward the bedroom. It was dark in there. I tried to put on the light, but I no longer remembered where the switch was located. This time, I nearly tripped over a chair.

It was the editor at my publisher's calling. A manuscript of mine had to go to press earlier than anticipated and if I wanted to see the final corrections, I had to come to New York at once. But in case I got to New York too late—this time of year it was sometimes impossible to get a flight immediately—the editor started reading me a number of errors, contradictions and inconsistencies in the text which he would have corrected first thing in the morning. In my urge to fix all these inaccuracies, which represented a potential danger to my literary career, I forgot all about my guest. When, a half hour later, I went back to the room where I'd left her, she'd already gone back to her own place. I knocked on her door but she didn't answer.

I flew to New York the next morning, and by the time I came back to Bal Harbour it was February. Priscilla Levy Clark had died. Others now lived in her apartments. What happened to the jade toilet seat, I never found out. Had the new tenant discovered that it was of jade and made a fortune on it? Maybe Priscilla had sold it, or maybe it was stolen when she was taken to the hospital.

Whenever I go into an antique store or attend an auction, I think that perhaps the toilet seat may turn up. Who knows—maybe some pauper found it in the garbage, installed it in his bathroom, and doesn't know that he sits each day on a treasure?

For me, this toilet seat became a symbol of sordid love, of the pursuit of wealth, of the passion for deceit, and of all worldly desires, ambitions, conceits.

"Leslie Aberdam," I murmur, "you were no more a slave than are others, and that which you left behind is more or less the same as we all shall leave when death is done with us."

Translated by Joseph Singer

A CAT IN STOCKINGS

There's an expression in the Talmud, "A crazy Hassid," which refers to a man who is so extremely religious, so anxious to keep all the laws of the Torah, that his piety borders on madness. Rabbi Isaiah Bechever, a distant relative of ours, was this kind of man. Among the most devout of Jews, there were those who took it upon themselves to recite one hundred blessings every day, including "Blessed be Thou O Lord our God, King of the Universe, Who brings forth bread from the earth," or "Who created the fruit of the vine," or many other such blessings over food and beverages. Even when a religious Jew went to the outhouse, he had to wash his hands and thank God for creating human in his wisdom and providing them with various openings for excrement and urine. Like all Orthodox Jewish men, Rabbi Isaiah blessed God early each morning for not being born a pagan, a female, or a slave. He blessed God when he wrapped himself in the prayer shawl and put the phylacteries on his head and arm. Three times a day, he recited the eighteen benedictions from his prayerbook. But altogether this still was far from a hundred. In his older years, Rabbi Isaiah suffered from trouble with his prostate, and had to urinate very often, reciting a blessing each time. But again, even these did not fill the quota. At times, when there was lightning and thunder during the day or night, he was given additional opportunities. Still, to recite one hundred blessings a day was a difficult undertaking. Had Rabbi Isaiah been able to eat and drink a great deal more, he might have been able to reach his goal. But Rabbi Isaiah fasted more than he ate.

Some time ago I happened to read a memoir written by a Catholic nun who made a similar vow, namely to chant the *Ave Maria* a specific number of times throughout the day and she had the same difficulties as Rabbi Isaiah. It seems that human nature and extreme religious devotion are essentially the same in all faiths. But let's return to Rabbi Isaiah.

Passover was for him a holiday rich with blessings. On the eve of Passover he had to recite a blessing as he removed the leavened bread from the house. Both on the first seder and the second, he had to recite blessings before he ate matzoh, the bitter herbs, the *afikoman*, and each time he drank one of the four glasses of wine. He had to bless the Almighty for delivering the Children of Israel from bondage in Egypt. If the first seder happened to fall on a Saturday night, he had to recite *Havdalah*, the prayer of separating between the holy Sabbath and the weekdays. Many days before Passover began, Rabbi Isaiah was assailed by fear that the slightest crumb of bread might be found in his house during the eight days of the holiday. He was particularly concerned that the cat, which his wife kept to catch mice, might drag in morsels of leavened bread stuck between her claws. He became so obsessed by this fear, that he hired a seamstress to sew four stockings to fit over the cat's paws. On Passover eve, his wife and daughters managed to put these stockings on the cat. Of course the cat was surprised by these strange events. It meowed and resisted. But how can you explain to an animal Rabbi Isaiah's dread and anxiety, and his intimate relations with God and His commandments? After a few Passovers, the cat grew accustomed to the idea that humans, the most clever creatures on earth, had whims that the feline brain could never grasp and that its only recourse was not to brood over it too much but simply to continue to live and catch mice, stockings or no stockings.

One Passover, something so bizarre happened – something so shocking and frightening – that Rabbi Isaiah and his family could never forget it to the very end of their lives. It was the first night of the seder, and Rabbi Isaiah was half-sitting, half-reclining, on his ceremonial chair, dressed in a white satin robe and a white skullcap embroidered with golden threads to give him the appearance of a king, which every Jew is supposed to look like on this night. His wife, the Rebbetzin, was dressed in a white silk gown, which had been a part of her wedding gifts, and a kerchief around her forehead studded with jewels, as befits a queen. One of Rabbi Isaiah's grandsons was asking the traditional Four Questions. and the rabbi answered him in the refrain from the Haggadah, "Slaves we were unto Pharaoh in Egypt, and the Lord our God brought us forth with an outstretched arm." The family all beamed with delight as their progeny sang out the Four Questions in Hebrew, and with what elation the rabbi told the story of our redemption from Egypt. The Rebbetzin and her daughters and granddaughters had prepared the holiday meal. Candles burned in the silver candlesticks. The first part of the Haggadah was completed. Rabbi Isaiah pointed to Elijah's cup, which was filled to the brim with wine, and he honored his youngest granddaughter with the privilege of opening the door to let Elijah the prophet in, even though nobody ever saw him enter or drink the wine. Suddenly the girl gasped and cried out. The cat darted inside the house without her stockings on, sprang onto the table and began to sniff the meat, fish, and matzah balls. The worst part of it all was that a bagel, the epitome of *hometz* – leavened bread – hung around her neck. Rabbi Isaiah leaped up and began to scream. The cat spilled Elijah's cup all over the festive tablecloth. The women burst into a mixture of wild screaming and convulsive laughter. The children tried to catch the cat by its tail, but it tore itself away. By some miracle, it didn't knock over the candlesticks and cause a fire. The cries were so great that the neighbors came running. Rabbi Isaiah was sure that only Satan and Asmodeus could have conspired in such a scheme to defile the seder and to contaminate the festive holiness of the house.

The cat itself seemed like a demon with its blazing eyes – one of the evil hosts. When things quieted down, the family began to suspect that this catastrophe was not really devised by demons and hobgoblins, but by the so-called "enlightened ones" in the village – a small group of atheists with whom Rabbi Isaiah had been waging war for years. It was they who tore off the cat's stockings and hung a bagel around its neck. The heretics rejoiced in making a mockery of Jewish life and religious Jews, whom they called "fanatics," "God's Cossacks," "bench-squeezers," and other such names.

One of the neighbors suddenly remembered that on one Passover night some years ago, the members of this malicious group had caught the community billygoat and pushed him into the house of a Hassid when the door was opened for Elijah. The cat could surely not have torn the stockings off by herself.

At first Rabbi Isaiah wanted to chase the cat out. True, a cat is an innocent creature, but since the ruffians and unbelievers used her to degrade this sacred night, it was better to get rid of her. But one of Rabbi Isaiah's sons-in-law reminded the rabbi of the story in the Talmud about the heretic Elisha, the son of Avihu, who used to ride a horse on the Sabbath and discuss Torah with his pupil, Rabbi Meir, who walked alongside the horse in order to hear the commentaries told by his master. Could one punish the horse because the spiteful Elisha was using it to break the laws of the Sabbath? Certainly not. The same reasoning may be applied to this cat, which always did exactly what she was created for – catch mice. After much debate, Rabbi Isaiah gave in. One of the neighbors, who was a shoemaker, promised next year to make the cat a pair of leather boots that could not be removed. After Rabbi Isaiah calmed down, he said, "Since these ungodly rebels have decided to wage war with the Almighty, we should, as the Talmud says, 'Let the owner of the vineyard clean out his vineyard.'" He sat down at the Passover table and began to chant the second part of the Haggadah, sure that the villains who committed this abomination would live to regret it. The Elijah's cup was filled again. The cat sat at the Rebbetzin's feet, as she always did at supper-time, and the benevolent Rebbetzin fed her leftovers from the meal – chicken, matzah balls, and other tidbits, as she did any other evening.

This story was told to me many years later by a granddaughter of Rabbi Isaiah. Her name was Hinda Reitza. She was present when the adventure with the cat took place. She said to me, "What do these creatures know about human beings, their intentions, their plans and complications?" Hinda Reitza had become "enlightened" herself in time and she said to me, "As you know, we finish reciting the Haggadah with a fable or a poem about a father who bought a sheep for two guldens. Then came a cat and ate up the sheep. Then came a dog and killed the cat. Then came a stick and hit the dog. Then came a fire and burned the stick. Then came water and extinguished the fire. Then came a butcher, who killed the ox. Then came the Angel of Death, who killed the butcher. Then came the Holy One, Who killed the Angel of Death. All this for no reason, no purpose, no real meaning. To me, this fable is the story of life – the life of animals and humans. This fable tells us: don't look for reason or justice, or for any sensible motivation or answer. We are all cats in stockings. We don't do things. Things are done to us. A celestial. Rabbi Isaiah sits in heaven as confused and perhaps as frightened as we are here on earth, and he's doing things to us which we can never understand or rectify. Why the editor of the Haggadah decided to include this playful almost juvenile fable in his collection was always a riddle to me. But is there anything which is not a riddle? It seems that the

Creator wanted to confuse his creatures from the very beginning and for ever after."

I'd met Hinda Reitza first in Paris in 1947, and then in Buenos Aires in 1957, and I've learned many facts from her about her grandfather, Rabbi Isaiah, and about my maternal grandfather, Rabbi Jacob Mordechai, whose son, my Uncle Isaac, married Rabbi Isaiah's daughter, Rachel.

Hinda Reitza told me many anecdotes about Rabbi Isaiah's extreme religiousness. Once she was traveling with him in a droshky in the city of Lublin to see a doctor. During the entire trip he kept screaming, "She's my granddaughter, she's my granddaughter, she's my granddaughter!" When she asked him why he was announcing this so many times and so loudly, he answered, "I don't want the whole world to think that I, Isaiah Bechever, am traveling with a woman I don't know, and take me as an example to indulge in sin." So devout was Rabbi Isaiah that his wife, Yente Perl, had to keep three sets of dishes: one for meat, one for dairy, and one for parve. For Passover she had another special set of dishes.

Wearing wigs over their shaved heads had become the new fashion for observant Jewish women in the big cities, but Rabbi Isaiah considered this an act of salacious vanity. It is written in the Talmud that the hair of a female evokes sinful thoughts in men, and a wig may arouse the same passions, Rabbi Isaiah argued. He had many disputes with his daughters and daughters-in-law about this issue. Some time later, wigs made of silk threads were invented, but Rabbi Isaiah condemned even this as a worldly trend, a compromise with evil. He said, "Whom are they trying to fool? Our Father in Heaven? In Heaven they know not only the deeds of every human being, but also his or her thoughts and intentions. It is written that a man does not scratch his finger if it is not decreed on High."

Hinda Reitza also told me that before he had become a rabbi, her grandfather was a scribe and wrote out Torah scrolls as well as *mezuzahs* and the inside scripts of phylacteries with a quill pen. He had made it his duty to immerse himself in the ritual bath each time before putting the name of God on parchment. He could never finish a Torah scroll since the name of God is mentioned thousands of times in the Hebrew Bible. Although he lived very close to the ritual bath, he spent years of his life walking there and then back home. The baths were generally occupied by women in the evenings, and if he was writing at night, he went to a nearby river and immersed himself there. If it happened to be winter, he plunged into the ice cold water. And since it is said that no harm is brought upon those who do God's bidding, Rabbi Isaiah lived to be ninety years of age.

On a visit to my grandfather, Rabbi Isaiah told him the story of the cat in stockings. Pious as my grandfather was, he also had a sense of humor and he said, "Not only cats can drag in crumbs of bread but also mice, and where will you find a seamstress to make stockings for mice? You are overdoing it, Rabbi. God does not demand so many precautions."

On this same visit, Rabbi Isaiah brought my grandfather a five hundred page manuscript in order to get a letter of approval from him, as was the custom. After reading the manuscript for some time, my grandfather reluctantly wrote the letter of approval and then said, "It is written in the Book of Psalms: 'Then shall the trees of the forest rejoice for the Lord is cometh to judge the earth.' It is agreed that the Psalmist was referring to the coming of the Messiah. The question is: Why should the trees be so joyful when the Messiah comes? What would they gain by it? The answer is: When the Messiah comes, the ovens will be heated with manuscripts instead of wood, and the trees will be exuberant to remain untouched.'" This was a gentle hint to Rabbi Isaiah that his writings did not belong to the very best.

Apropos the Messiah, my mother, the daughter of that witty rabbi, once told me that it is written somewhere that when the

Messiah comes, all the sick will be healed, except the fools. Why? The sick people, she explained, will know that they are sick and they will pray to God to be healed, and God will answer their prayers. The fools will consider themselves great sages, will not pray for any cure, and will remain what they were for the rest of their lives.

Extremists of Rabbi Bechever's kind are not only to be found among religious people but also among atheists. I would say that they are "religious" in their atheism. There were Jewish anarchists who considered it an atheistic *mitzvah* to organize a ball every year on Yom Kippur, just to spite the religious Jews and perhaps the Almighty too. The Hassidim joked about these ardent disbelievers, saying that they ate nails cooked in pig's fat.

Apropos the atheists, according to the Talmud, one is not allowed to matzah before Passover. The Talmud compares a man who eats matzah before Passover to a groom who lives with his bride before the wedding. Once, an atheist came to a rabbi and said, "Rabbi, I have committed both of these transgressions, and I must say that there is no comparison whatsoever!"

Translated by the author

JOB

Being a writer for a Yiddish newspaper means wasting half the workday on people who come to request advice or simply to argue. The manager, Mr. Raskin, tried several times to bring this custom to an end but failed repeatedly. Readers had each time broken in by force. Others warned that they would picket the editorial office. Hundreds of protest letters arrived in the mail.

In one case, the person in question didn't even knock. He threw open the door and I saw a tiny man wearing a black coat that was too long and too wide, a pair of loose-hanging gray pants that seemed ready to fall off at any moment, a shirt with an open collar and no tie, and a small black spot-stained hat poised high over his brow. Patches of black and white hair sprouted over his sunken cheeks, crawling all the way down to the bottom of his neck. His protruding eyes—a mixture of brown and yellow—looked at me with open mockery. He spoke with the singsong of Torah study:

"Just like this? Without a beard? With bared head? Considering your scribbling, I thought that you sit here covered in prayer shawl and phylacteries like the Vilna Gaon—forgive the comparison—and that between each sentence you immerse yourself in a ritual bath. Oh, I know, I know, religion is just a fad for you writers. For you little writers religion is just a fashion. You have to give the stupid public what it wants."

A wise guy, I thought. Aloud I said, "Please, sit down."

"And what good would it do me to sit down? Let me first get a good look at you. Here you do your writing? At this little table you fabricate your merchandise? Here you get your so-called inspiration? Well, and how were all the other lies written? Just with pen and ink. Paper is patient. You can even write that there's a horse fair in Heaven."

"What's your name?" I asked.

"My name is Koppel Stein, but you can call me Job, because I've suffered as much as Job, and, perhaps, a little extra for good measure. Job had three friends who came to comfort him, and in the end God himself spoke to him. And He ginally repaid him twice over: more donkeys, prettier daughters, and who knows what else. Nobody wants to comfort me and the Almighty remains silent, as if nothing had happened. I'm Job squared, if one can put it this way. Do you have a match? I've forgotten my matches."

I went out and brought him matches. He lit a cigarette and blew the smoke right in my face.

"Forgive me for speaking this way. As they say, it's my troubles speaking. You know the Talmud well: 'blame not a man in his hour of sorrow.' Some time ago you complained in an article about a reader who'd held you up for six straight hours. I'll keep it short, though how can one shorten a story that's already lasted more than forty years? I'll give you just the plain facts and if you're no fool it'll be as they say: 'a word to the wise is enough.' I'm one of those crazy people – this, it seems, is what you called them – who want to save the world, to bring justice, and other such improbable things. With me it started when I was still a little kid. Our neighbor Tevel, the shoemaker, used to work from daybreak to late at night. In the winter I heard him hammering in nails when it was still dark outside. He lived in a tiny room which served as everything: the kitchen, the bedroom, the workshop. There his wife, Necha, gave birth every nine or ten months, and there the infants died. My father wasn't much richer. He was a teacher. We lived in one room, too, and had so little to eat that we might as well have deposited our teeth in the bank. Early on I began to ask: How is this possible? My father answered that this was God's will and I came to despise – to really hate – the all-powerful God who sat eternally in his seventh heaven, surrounded by honors and glory, while his creatures were tortured to death. I won't get into details – I know from your work that you know these details yourself and even the so-called psychology.

"In short, I was about fifteen when I became a disbeliever. We formed a political group in town where we read Karl Marx, Kautsky, and even got our hands on a brochure by Lenin – in Russian, not in Yiddish. In 1917, when the Revolution broke out, I was a Russian soldier. I was even wounded near Przemysl and was confined to a military hospital. What I went through in the barracks and on the front you probably know yourself. No, you don't, because my greatest troubles came from my own mouth. I told everyone what I considered to be the truth. I talked back to the officers. To this day I don't know why they didn't court-martial me and have me shot. They just needed cannon fodder.

"Kerensky told us to continue fighting for beloved Mother Russia and I became a Bolshevik. I was one even before that. I ended up in Poltava, and there we experienced the October Revolution. An army loyal to the Czar attacked us and drove us from place to place. Who didn't attack us? Denikin, Petliura, many others. I was wounded again and the Red Army let me go. I got stuck in a village where there were pogroms against the Jews. With my own eyes I saw children slaughtered. I lay in the hospital with gangrene in one foot. I'll never understand why, out of everyone, I came out alive. Around me people were dying from typhoid fever and all kinds of other sicknesses. For me, death had become an everyday occurrence. Just the same, my faith in human progress became stronger, not weaker. Who started wars? Capitalists. Who incited pogroms? They did. I'd seen plenty of wickedness, idiocy, and pettiness among my own comrades, but ten times a day I answered myself with the same refrain: we are products of the capitalist system. Socialism will produce a new humanity – and so on and so forth. Meanwhile, my parents died in Poland, my father from hunger and my mother from typhoid fever. Or perhaps she, too, died of starvation.

"After the counter-revolutionary mobs were driven out and things some kind of order was established, I decided to become a laborer, even though I could have taken a government job or even become a commissar. By that time I was in Moscow. I'd studied carpentry in our little town not I got a job in a furniture factory. Lenin was still alive. For the masses, it was still a holiday. The NEP – the New Economic Policy – did not disappoint us. How do the Hassidim put it? 'Descent for the sake of ascent.' Standing and listening to Lenin give a speech was compensation enough for all the pain and humiliation. In the factory where I worked they cursed me and called me a 'dirty Jew' and mocked me no less than they did in the Czarist barracks. They played all kinds of tricks on me – and who did it? Party members, fellow workers, Communists. At every opportunity they told me me to go back to Palestine. True, I could have complained. There were cases of workers being sent to prison for antisemitic actions. But I soon realized that these were not isolated incidents. The whole factory was permeated with hatred – and not only toward the Jews. A Tartar was as much of a target, and when the Russians felt like it, they made mincemeat of the Ukrainians, Belarusians, and Poles. How can you clean out a garbage dump? I saw with shame that the Revolution changed nothing. It was all the same: drunkenness, debauchery, intrigues, theft, sabotage. A doubt crept into my mind, but I repressed it with all my strength. After all, things were just beginning.

"I promised you to be short and this is what I'll do. Lenin died. Stalin took over. Then came the plot against Trotsky

– who for me was a god. Suddenly I hear that he is nothing but a spy, a lackey working for Pilsudski, Leon Blum, MacDonald, Rockefeller. There are hearts that burst from the least worries, and other hearts that are as like stones. I must have a stone on my left side. What I've put up with I could only wish on Hitler – if it's true that he's still alive somewhere in Spain or Argentina. I shared a room – actually a cell – with two other workers: drunkards, outcasts. The obscenities they used – the filth! They stole from my pockets. In the factory, they called me Trotsky. And the 'r' they pronounced with a Jewish accent. Then came the arrests and purges. People I knew – idealists – were taken to prison and either got sent off to Siberia or else rotted in jail. I began to realize, to my horror, that Trotsky was right. The Revolution had been betrayed.

"But what can you do concretely? Could Russia endure a new revolution, or even a permanent revolution? Can a sick body stand one operation after another? As my mother, peace be with her, used to say: 'If a dog licked my blood, it would be poisoned.'

"This way years passed. Permanent revolution is impossible, but permanent despair exists. I went to sleep in despair and got up in despair. I was drained of all hope. Still, despite the persecution, Trotskyist circles did spring up. The old conspiracies from the Czarist times returned. The Revolution had fallen flat. But humankind cannot become resigned. This is its misfortune."

"In 1928, I returned to Poland. It's easier said than done. I smuggled myself across the border, helped by fellow-Trotskyites. Each step involved the greatest of dangers. I forgot to tell you that while still in Russia I'd been imprisoned in the Lubyanka for seven months precisely, just on the suspicion of being a Trotskyite. Not a night passed that I wasn't beaten. Do you see this crippled fingernail? A Chekist pierced it with a glowing needle. They knocked out my teeth – and it was all done by my proletarian brothers. A curse upon humanity! What went on in jail cannot be described. People were physically and spiritually ruined. The stench of the urinals drove you insane. The prisoners were not all political. There was homosexuality and there was outright rape. I went though all this before I smuggled myself into Poland at the town of Nieśwież. The moment I crossed the border the Poles arrested me. After a few weeks let me out and then they put me into jail again. This was in 1930. In Russia, I'd been given a contact among the Trotskyites in Warsaw, but they were all poor young men, simple workers. The Stalinists considered it a good deed to denounce the Trotskyites to the Polish authorities, and most of them sat in Pawiak or Wronki – a terrible prison. In Warsaw, I tried to tell them about what was going on in Russia, and the young little Stalinists, the former yeshiva boys and simple idlers, hounded me so that I longed for Russia. I was beaten, spat on, and called a renegade, a fascist, a traitor. A few times I tried to speak to an audience, but the underworld thugs from Krochmalna and Smocza Street silenced me with stones and rotten eggs. Once I was even stabbed with a knife. There's no worse cynic than a Jewish Chekist or Jewish Communist. They spit on the truth. They're ready to kill and torture you at the slightest suspicion. I saw already then that there was no difference between Communists and Nazis. But I still believed that Trotskyism was better. Something had to be good. Not everyone could be evil.

"Until now I haven't mentioned my personal life because I didn't have one in Russia. Even if I wanted to sin, there was no opportunity. With three or four men living in a single room, you'd have to be an exhibitionist. I witnessed the shame and disgrace of both sexes and I lost my appetite. After the Revolution, hundreds of thousands of illegitimate children, the so-called Bezdomniks, were roaming the streets, and they became a curse and a danger for Russia. When a woman went to buy bread, they fell upon her and stole it from her. Very often they raped her too. There was no lack of thieves, murderers, drunkards. The Revolution was supposed to make an end to prostitution, but prostitutes loitered around the Kremlin. In Warsaw, I met a Trotskyist woman. She was hunchbacked, but for me a physical defect is no drawback. She seemed quick, intelligent, idealistic. The sorrow and also the wisdom fo the world looked out from her black eyes – though what wisdom does the world possess? We became close. Neither of us thought much of going to a rabbi. We rented an attic room on Smocza Street and there we began to live together. That's also where we had our daughter, Rosa. Naturally, we named her after Rosa Luxemburg.

"My wife, Sonia, was a trained nurse and she often spent her nights at the homes of the sick. We rarely had a night together. I couldn't get work in the Polish shops and made a few zlotys repairing poor people's furniture – a cupboard, a table, a bed. I earned, as they say, water for the groats. As long as there was no child we managed. But as Sonia's pregnancy advanced things became bad. Just then I was arrested. My Jewish proletarian brothers had placed illicit literature in my home and denounced me to the police. You will never know what people are capable of doing. Many of them were killed in the Spanish Civil War, shot by their own comrades. Others died years later in Stalin's purges and slave camps.

"The entire trial against me was a wild invention. Everyone knew it: the judge, the prosecutor, the police. They accused me of conspiring against the Polish Republic with people people whose faces I'd never seen. The policemen, upholders of the law, bore false witness against me and swore to lies. In prison, the Stalinists tortured me so that every day was hell. Among the rich there were do-gooders who brought political prisoners food, cigarettes, other things. They hired lawyers free of change. But since I didn't believe in Comrade Stalin, I was as good as excommunicated. My fellow prisoners played nasty tricks on me. They tore my books, put dirt in my soup, literally spat on me a hundred times a day. I stopped talking altogether and went silent – deaf and mute. In order not to hear their abuse and curses, I used to stuff my ears with soft bread or cotton from my coat. They harassed me even at night, all in the name of Socialism: a bright future, a better tomorrow, and all their other slogans. The tortured became torturers. Don't think that I still have any illusions about the Trotskyists. I've realized one thing: the worst scum comes from those who want to make a better world. If there are some decent people, they are to be found among simple folk – merchants, tradesmen, shopkeepers. But among those who want to bring about the coming of the Red Messiah there is no truth and no compassion. What's can be more convenient than tormenting others in the name of an ideal? It got to the point that the Polish prison guards began to defend me and plead that I be left in peace. I asked them to be placed among the criminals. And when my request was granted, the comrades exploited it to demonstrate and protest that a political prisoner had been put among thieves and cutthroats. They wanted to keep me for themselves. This is how they behaved – people who were supposedly fighting for justice.

"Sitting among the thieves, pimps, and murderers was hardly pleasurable. They eyed me with suspicion. There was an old animosity between the criminals and the socialists which dated to 1905. But in comparison with what I endured from the Stalinists, this was paradise. True, my new inmates stole my cigarettes and made off with portions of the packages that Sonia sent me, but they let me read my books in peace. Instead of 'fascist,' they called me 'idiot,' and this hurt less. It sometimes happened that a thief or a pimp would offer me a piece of sausage or a cigarette. What was there for them to do in the cell? Either you play cards, which were marked and stained, or you talked. From the stories

I heard there, one could write ten books. And their Yiddish! The comrades spoke the Yiddish of their cheap pamphlets. It was not a language but some kind of jargon. But the criminals spoke the real juicy mother tongue. They used words and expressions that astounded me. It's a shame I didn't write them down! Well, and their opinions about the world! They had a philosophy of their own.

"When I went to prison, I had still believed in the revolution, in Karl Marx. I still had some political aspirations. Back outside I was completely cured. While I sat in jail, disappointment in Stalin grew in Poland. Things had reached the point that the Communist Party of Poland was dissolved by the Comintern. Many of my persecutors had gone to the 'land of socialism' – where they were liquidated. I was told about one idiot who, having crossed the border, fell down on his knees and started kissing the earth, just as ancient Jews did when arriving in the Land of Israel. As he lay down kissing the red mud, two border guards approached and arrested him. He was sent to dig gold in the north, and there even a giant didn't last longer than a year. This was the way the Communist Party treated those who'd sacrificed themselves for the cause.

"Then a new curse wriggled its way in: Nazism. It was Communism's rightful heir. Hitler had learned all his methods from the Reds: the concentration camps, the liquidations, the mass murders. When I got out of prison in 1934 and told Sonia what I thought about our little world and those who wanted to save it, she berated me like the worst of them. The truth is that while I languished behind bars, I'd become a kind of martyr or hero for the Trotskyists in Warsaw. I could have played the role of a great leader but I spoke to them clearly: children, there is no cure for the human tragedy. It's not the fault of the 'system' but of *Homo sapiens* itself. When they heard such heresy they became outraged. Sonia et me know that she refused to live with a renegade. I had the luck of becoming a renegade twice over. Besides, while I was in prison, she had lived with another man. Hunchbacks are hot-blooded and there's always a volunteer handy. He was a simple fellow from the provinces, I think he was a barber. Little Rosa called him *papa*."

"Don't look so frightened! I won't keep you here until morning. I think you left for America in 1935 and you don't know what happened in Poland after that. There was a complete collapse. Stalinists became Trotskyists, while Trotskyists joined the Polish Socialist Party or the Bund. Others turned Zionists. I myself tried religion. I entered a study house and sat down to pore over a volume of the Talmud, but for this one needs faith, otherwise it's just nostalgia. The anarchists raised their heads again. Some still believed in Kropotkin, others followed Stirner. We had guests in Poland, Ridz-Szmigli had invited Nazis to hunt in the Białowieża Forest. Then came the Stalin-Hitler pact and the War. When the Germans began to bombard Warsaw most of our able bodied men ran over the Praga Bridge and set out for Russia. Some of them still had hopes about the Soviet Union but I knew where I was going. Yet staying among the Nazis was not an option. I came to say goodbye to Sonia and found her in bed with the barber. Little Rosa started crying, 'Papa, take me with you!' These cries follow me still. They haunt me at night. They all perished.

"I was present in Bialystok when many of Yiddish writers from Poland suddenly turned into ardent Stalinists. Some even denounced their own colleagues. I was known as a Trotskyist and I was headed for certain death, but by then I'd arrived at a kind of philosophy. We cannot live a straight life. We can only be smugglers, runners, deserters. People, like beasts, must constantly hide. If the enemy's on the right, you go left. He goes left, you creep to the right. This philosophy – you may call it cowardice – helped me. I knew where the informers were and I avoided them. Many leftists, half-leftists, and converted leftists went to Vilna or Kovno, but I went on to Russia, not to the big cities, but to little towns, villages, *kolkhozes*. There I found different Russians: generous, ready to help. They laughed at communism.

"Until 1941, I managed somehow. When the war arrived in Russia, so did starvation. Refugees on foot poured in by the millions. Others were brought in freight trains. Millions of Russians went to the front. I starved, slept in railway stations, passed through all seven circles of Gehenna. But one thing I avoided: prison. I kept my mouth shut, played the role of a simple person, half-illiterate. I worked where I could. On the *kolkhozes* and in factories I saw what communist economy meant. Machines were broken, raw materials was wasted. It couldn't even be called sabotage. It was simply a beastly indifference to anything that didn't directly relate to them. The whole system was such that you either stole or you died. I went into a factory and the bookkeeper, a young man from Warsaw, did the accounting on books by Chekhov, Gogol, Tolstoy. On the margins of the pages and between the lines he scribbled his figures – obviously false. Notepaper was not available. People lived on stolen food which was sold on the black market. You couldn't imagine it unless you saw it with your own eyes. If not for America – and had the Nazis not been such cruel murderers – Hitler would have reached Vladivostok.

"I didn't live – I smuggled myself through life. I became a worm, I crawled here, I crept there. As long they didn't crush me, I kept on crawling. I saw to my amazement that the whole country was like this. We became like the lice that infested us. Until I came to Russia for the second time I still had some romanticism in me, a sexual morality. But later I lost this too. Millions of men were scattered on the fronts and their wives lived with anyone they could find. I slept with women whose names I didn't know. In the dark I had females whose faces I never saw. I remember lying with a woman on rotten hay in a barn. She gave herself to me and cried. I asked her, 'Why are you crying?' And she moaned, 'If Grishenka knew! Where is he, my little eagle? What have I done to him!' And she pressed herself to me, wailing. She said, 'You're not a man to me but a candle for masturbation.' Suddenly she began to kiss me and wet me with her tears. 'What do I have against you? You, too, probably left someone dear – a curse on fascism!'

"In Tashkent I got typhoid fever complicated later by pneumonia. I lay in a hospital and around me people were dying. Some Pole spoke to me and told me about all his plans. Then he went silent. I answered him and he didn't respond. The nurse entered and he was dead. Just like that, in the middle of a sentence. He suffered from scurvy or beriberi, and with such diseases people died, so to speak, without an introduction. I grew indifferent to death. I wouldn't have believed it possible.

"Don't think that I came here just to bother you and tell you my life story. Since I'm here, this means that I've managed to smuggle myself through everything – hunger, epidemics, murder, ruin, borders. Now, as you see, I'm in the United States. I already have citizenship papers. I've already been mugged in your America and they pointed a gun at my chest. Another refugee, who crossed on the same ship, has raised himself to the position of a factory owner in New York. He immediately forgot all the deaths, all the murders, and began to do business. I recently met him in a cafeteria and he complained to me that his stocks had fallen. He married a woman who'd lost her husband and children, but they already have new children. I talk about smuggling myself, but he's a real smuggler. He was already smuggling in the German Displaced Persons Camp, where he waited for an American visa.

"Wait, why did I come to you? Yes, I came with an idea. I beg you, don't laugh at me."

"What's this idea?"

He paused for a while and lit another cigarette.

"You'll think I'm crazy," he said. "My idea is that all decent people to commit suicide."

"Is that so?"

"You laugh? It's nothing to laugh about. I'm not the only one disappointed in the human species. There are millions like me. Since all hope is gone, why suffer for nothing? I read your works while still in Warsaw. I read you here too. You are the only one who offers no hope to humanity. Lately you've started praising religion. But your religion is one of resignation. You always come to the same conclusion: this is God's will. But maybe God wants humanity to put an end to it all. I beg you, don't interrupt me! There are scores of different religions and cults. Why shouldn't there be a movement that preaches suicide? How long will we go on smuggling ourselves through life, only to be crushed in the end? My feeling is that very many people are ready to end everything, but they lack the courage – the last push. If millions of idiots were willing to die for Hitler and Stalin and all kinds of other maniacs, why shouldn't people want to perish as a protest? We must throw back at God's gift back at Him – this abominable struggle for existence, which anyhow ends in defeat. First of all, people must stop having children, bringing into the world new victims. Let the scumbags hope, let them fight for bread, sex, prestige, for the fatherland, for Communism, and for all kinds of other isms. If a remnant of spirit remains in humanity, it should come to the conviction that all this swinish filth isn't worthwhile."

"My dear friend," I said, "suicide can never become a mass movement."

"How can you be so sure? What was the Battle of Verdun if not mass suicide?"

"There they hoped for victory."

"What victory? They sent a hundred thousand soldiers into battle and ended up with sixty thousand graves."

"Some survived. Some received medals."

"Maybe they should create a suicide medal."

"You're still a worldsaver," I said. "Suicide is committed alone, not with partners."

"I read somewhere that in America they have suicide clubs."

"For the rich, not the poor."

He laughed and showed a toothless grin. He spat out his cigarette butt and stamped it out.

"So what should I do?" he asked. "Become rich? Perhaps I should. It would, after all, be like Job."

Translated by the author, Dorothea Straus, and David Stromberg

MENDEL I THOUGHT

Isaac Bashevis Singer

In the *heder* that I attended in Warsaw, there was a boy, Mendel whose nickname was "I Thought." That's what the boys called him and the reason was that he made countless mistakes for which he always had the same answer: "I thought..." For instance, one time, as winter approached, he tried to slide over the sewer in front of our heder. The real frosts hadn't yet started and the sewer was merely covered by a thin layer of ice. Mendel took off running and sank knee-deep into the cold dirty water. The other boys managed to pull him out. When they asked him why he had attempted to slide over such thin ice, he said, "I thought the ice was thicker."

"Why didn't you test the ice with a stick?" the boys asked, and Mendel replied, "I thought I didn't need to..."

"When *you* think, you end up fooling yourself!" the heder boys exclaimed together.

Streetcar 22 ran through Mendel's street, but he often boarded other lines and strayed off to strange and far-off neighborhoods. When asked why he'd taken the wrong line, he replied, "I thought it was number twenty-two." On one holiday, Mendel drank some ink. He had seen a bottle of red liquid, poured himself a glassful, and gulped it down. When asked why, his answer was, "I thought it was borsht."

His parents suspected that something was wrong with Mendel's eyes and took him to an eye doctor, but it turned out that he had exceptionally good vision. His problem was that he never stopped to consider anything, always acting in haste. His blunders were often incredibly funny. He wanted to buy rolls and went into a haberdashery. When the haberdasher pointed out his mistake, Mendel said, "I thought it was a bakery."

His father gave him letters to post, but Mendel threw them into a garbage can. Weeks later, when they found out what he'd done, he said, "I thought it was a mailbox."

On Sabbaths there was no heder, but every few weeks or so, Mendel would show up there on a Saturday morning. The heder was connected to the teacher's house. Mendel would knock on the door carrying not only his Hebrew Bible and prayer book, but his notebooks, pens, and pencils, too, objects that are forbidden to handle on the Sabbath. His answer was, "I thought it was Friday," or, "I thought it was Monday."

One time he came to heder wearing his sister's red beret. His answer: "I thought it was my cap."

A day didn't go by in heder that Mendel didn't mistake some other boy's Bible, prayer book, notebook, or pen for his own. In winter, he regularly picked up the wrong overcoat, galoshes, or gloves. He also mixed up everyone's names. Mendel had a dark friend whose name was Velvel, but Mendel often came up to me and addressed me as if I were Velvel. I was as fair-skinned as Velvel was dark and, besides, I had red hair. As if this weren't enough, Velvel was taller and broader than I, and I could never understand how Mendel could mistake me for Velvel. Still, he kept doing this, and each time he'd say, "I thought you were Velvel."

Not only did Mendel commit blunders, he caused actual harm to himself. One time his parents took him to a hotel that had a glass door. Mendel went charging into the glass door because he thought there was nothing there, and bruised his forehead and nose. A few times he walked into a mirror.

Mendel's parents lived on the third floor of their building, but he would go home from heder and knock on the door of the second-floor apartment. When the woman who lived there opened the door, he called her Mama and began telling her what happened that day at the heder with such haste that it took several minutes before she could manage to point out his error. Then he said, "Oh, I thought you were my mother."

Boys joked in the heder that when Mendel grew up and got married, he wouldn't recognize his own wife. Others said that he would mistake himself for someone else. In connection with this, our teacher told us the story of the absent-minded scholar who came in from the street where it was raining hard. Instead of placing his umbrella by the door in the hallway and going inside to warm up by the stove, he put the umbrella near the stove and stationed himself by the hallway door.

I met Mendel 30 years later in America. When he told me that he was a physics professor and involved in research calling for the utmost accuracy and precision, I said, "Mendel, I thought you'd grow up a schlemiel."

Mendel smiled, winked and said, "If you think, you fool yourself."

Still, when we went to a café together, I observed Mendel pouring salt into his coffee.

I said, "Mendel, that's salt!"

He glanced at me in confusion and said, "I thought it was sugar."

"Mendel," I went on, "you're wearing one red sock and one black one."

"You're right. I thought they were the same."

He seemed to grow embarrassed and asked, "Do you smoke, Velvel? Here, have a European cigarette."

"I'm Isaac," I replied, "not Velvel. And I don't smoke."

"In that case, I'll have one myself."

He took out a cigarette and stuck it in his mouth, but with the tip facing out, and tried to light the filter with a lighter. The lighter wouldn't work, and he handed it to me to try.

I examined it and said, "You've filled it with perfume instead of lighter fluid."

"Oh, I thought it was lighter fluid. Maybe you have a match?"

"Yes, but first turn your cigarette around, so that I can light the tobacco instead of the filter."

He turned the cigarette around and lit it from my match.

"I've conducted hundreds of experiments in the laboratory without a single error. I'm considered one of the best researchers in America. Do you understand this? Wait, I'll order more coffee."

He stopped a woman passing by, and said, "Another coffee, and apple cake!"

The woman smiled. "I'm not the waitress."

"Oh, sorry, I thought you were the waitress."

"It doesn't matter."

And she walked toward the exit.

"Mendel, you haven't changed a bit," I observed.

We drank the coffee. When the waitress came with the check, I reached for it, but Mendel snatched it first.

"Velvel," he said, "you're my guest. Let me pay."

As we were leaving, I noticed that Mendel was arguing with the cashier. It seemed that instead of the check, he had handed the cashier his business card.

When we finally went outside, Mendel stuck his hand into his pocket and suddenly cried, "This isn't my coat!"

I waited outside for him to get his coat. We walked and he complained, "Velvel, you still haven't answered my question. In my work, I never make a mistake. I discovered an element that exists only for a hundredth of a millionth of a second. To do this, you have to be incredibly precise... Please, Velvel, I beg you on all that's holy to come home with me. I want to introduce you to my wife. I've often spoken of you to her and she's read everything you've written. It will be a great surprise for her. Taxi!"

Mendel raised his arms and began waving them frantically.

A police car pulled up.

"What is it, sir?" a policeman asked.

"Oh, I thought you were a taxi!"

We laughed and Mendel took my arm.

"You still haven't answered my question. Taxi!"

"Why didn't he stop?" Mandel asked.

"Because he was already carrying three passengers."

"I thought it was empty. Velvel, what's the answer to my question?"

"The answer is that my name is Isaac, not Velvel. Is Velvel a writer, too?" I asked.

"Velvel is a dentist and he lives in London, not here in Washington."

"This is New York, not Washington," I said.

"I meant New York. Taxi!"

This time the taxi stopped and we got in.

When the taxi pulled up to the building, Mendel exclaimed, "This isn't my house!"

"That's the address you gave me, sir," the driver said. "Two-Ten West Sixty-First Street."

"I live on East Sixty-first Street, not West."

"You said West."

"I meant East."

"So we'll go east!"

And the driver headed that way.

For a long time, we didn't speak, then Mendel said, "You mustn't think I'm always this absent-minded. But when I saw you,

Velvel, I got completely distracted. Where are my glasses? I don't have my glasses! And where is my fountain pen? Well, it's one of those days. But it's all been worth it! Where's my briefcase?"

"You didn't have a briefcase with you," I said.

"What? Thank God! I thought I had lost my briefcase, too. Come, my mother is waiting."

"Your mother is alive – and here in America?" I asked.

"I meant my wife."

"Mendel, you are absolutely the same!"

"And so are you, Velvel," he answered. "You haven't changed a bit."

I was soon introduced to Mendel's wife, a charming woman, and the first words she said to him were, "You forgot your glasses and fountain pen on your desk."

Mendel shrugged.

"I thought I lost them on the bus."

Translated by Joseph Singer

THE MURDERER

They all knew him although no one in Bałtów spoke to him and he spoke to no one. Maryan Skiba had served a prison term of eight years for killing his girl- friend, Zocha, because he caught her in bed with a city hall official. Maryan was a fisherman. After his release from the Lublin prison he returned to his former trade. There was a lake around Bałtów that had carp, pike, and tench. It belonged to a nobleman who permitted the fishermen to fish there for a fee. All day Thursday, and Friday until noon, Maryan would stand in the marketplace beside his tub of live fish. It was impossible to haggle with him, as he had almost stopped talking. He muttered the cost and no one could get another word out of him. His price was slightly lower than the other fishmongers' and he gener- ally sold his catch. Sometimes when there were more fish than customers, the others lowered their prices, but not Maryan. It was said that he threw the unsold fish back into the water.

He inherited a hut not far from the Catholic cemetery and there he lived alone. Around his property he had built a fence so that the apprentice tailors and shoemakers who passed by on Saturdays with the maids and seamstresses on their way to the forest could not look into his windows. He kept a dog, a cat, a parrot, and a goldfish in a glass bowl. On the wall above his head hung a hunter's gun, a sword, and the stuffed head of a boar.

Maryan Skiba, short and squat, had a square head that rested on his shoulders almost without a neck. His flaxen hair reached to the middle of his forehead and stood up like a hog's bristles. He had a red face, a snub nose with flared nostrils, and round yellow eyes without brows. When Maryan came back to Bałtów the priest sent for him and tried to make him join the church, quoting from the Bible that the merciful God has pity on his erring flock. But Maryan replied, "There is no God." And he refused further discussions.

The matchmaker Tekla Kalupek, a widow, tried to match Maryan with a girl from a nearby province, an orphan. Maryan listened to the matchmaker without blinking an eye. Then he said, "I don't want to marry."

"A man needs a wife."

"I'm not a man."

"What are you?"

"A murderer."

Since then he'd been avoided by everyone. He, too, avoided everyone, even refusing to have any business with the other fishermen. If they spread their nets on one part of the shore, he went to another. There was talk that he copulated with a she-demon. Once some boys climbed over his fence and peeped through his window. They saw him sitting on a tree stump, mending a net. He seemed to eat only fish because he never came to any store to buy food, though he grew some vegetables in his garden.

His pets were trained to play together and taught not to harm one another. Dymniak the letter carrier swore that once, when he brought Maryan a letter from a former inmate, he saw a cat riding on the dog's back, and on the tail of the cat perched a small yellow bird. This had only one meaning, that Maryan was a sorcerer.

Actually Maryan Skiba had learned to train animals from a bear trainer by the name of Stach, who shared his cell for many years. Stach had murdered a boy because he stole a copper three-kopeck coin from him. Stach could tell fortunes from cards like a gypsy. One day a crow had flown through the iron bars and Stach taught him to speak. Stach boasted that he was a mind reader and that by the sheer power of thinking he could command his animals to do his bidding. He told Maryan that he awakened in the middle of the night and that some part of him, a spirit, emerged from his body. It left the prison, flew over the Lublin streets, and then above fields, rivers, forests, far from the city. Stach had left behind a mistress, Karola, a magician who could eat fire, swallow knives, and roll a barrel in the air, balanced on the soles of her feet. During his night wanderings, Stach's spiritual half met Karola and made love to her.

Now that Maryan was free, he tried to practice what Stach had taught him. He never succeeded in flying during the night, except in his dreams, but he was remarkably successful with living creatures. Without uttering a word he commanded Burek, his dog, to bark three times, and he did just that. In the same way he made Duszka the cat lick Burek's ear. Once a wandering circus came to Bałtów and Maryan attended every performance. From one of the performers Maryan bought two greenish birds, a pair, which belonged to the parrot family though they were not much bigger than sparrows. Maryan named the male Stach and the female Karola. Stach could say a few words and Maryan taught him new ones and even a little song. Maryan built a nest with hay and leaves for the couple and Karola soon began to lay eggs and sit on them. For the growing family, Maryan braided a large cage.

Karola did not show much inclination to learn, but Stach was a diligent pupil. He became more attached to Maryan than to his wife. He often stood on Maryan's head, jabbered, whistled, pulled at his earlobe, and spoke tick- lish secrets to him. When Maryan mended a net, Stach settled on the index finger of his right hand. Maryan had developed so much confidence in Stach that during the summer, when he sold his fish in the marketplace, he let Stach perch on his shoulder, and the bird never flew away.

Stach's devotion to Maryan became greater from day to day. He fought with the other males, his sons and grandsons. Small as he was, he began a war with the larger parrot. Stach could not stand to see Maryan pet the cat or caress the dog. He screeched with a voice that was hard to believe could come from such a tiny creature. How strange that the other birds and even the cat and the dog were afraid of Stach and his shrill reproaches. Often when Stach went into a rage, the old parrot entered his cage and leaned his head to one side, and his golden eye seemed to ask, Why is he so upset? The cat hid under the bed. The dog slunk into the corner, his tail between his legs. Sometimes, when Stach was displeased, he flew back and forth, hitting against the walls and windows and scold- ing in bird language. He even tried to bite the other pets. One night when Maryan awoke and could not fall asleep again, a strange idea occurred to him: that the soul of the murdered Zocha had entered Stach. In all these years Maryan could never forget Zocha, the love she gave him in the beginning of their relationship, the sweet talk, and the wails she let out when he walked in with an ax in his hand to confront her in bed with her seducer. Maryan began to imagine that he heard Zocha's voice in Stach. The love the bird showed him was not natural. Zocha must have forgiven him and returned from the other world.

Maryan sometimes called Stach, Zocha. He quickly responded to that name and repeated it at once.

The Zocha that was in Stach decided to destroy all competition. Burek, the dog, for no apparent reason, stopped eating and snapped at his mas- ter. Burek had a fight with a porcupine and came home with a snout full of quills. Maryan tried to remove them but Burek resisted and howled as though he had gone mad. He uttered a last bark and fell dead. One afternoon the cat climbed up to the windowsill and sat curled up between the flowerpots. When Maryan called her to eat she did not respond. The cat had expired. A few weeks later the parrot died. At dawn one morning Maryan heard screaming from the cage where Stach and his family slept at night. The cage was covered with a shawl that had once been Zocha's. Maryan wondered. As a rule birds kept quiet when it was dark. He wanted to get up to see what happened but he was so exhausted from work that his head fell back on the pillow like a stone. At daybreak when Maryan awoke it occurred to him that it was unusually quiet. He rose from his cot. All the birds in the cage were dead except for Stach. He was perched on a stick and looked down at the carcasses, his beak bloody. Feathers and down were scattered every- where. Stach had killed his clan. It is Zocha's revenge, Maryan murmured. Then he yelled, "Murderer."

Stach flew out of the cage, screamed with a human voice, hit windowpanes, shelves, rafters. In his outburst he dislocated his wing. Maryan tried to snap it back for him, but Stach remained a cripple.

From that day on, Maryan never brought another creature into the house. He locked Stach in the cage for a period of eight weeks, for the eight years he himself had spent in jail. The bird was never the same again after his release. All day long he stood on the roof of his cage with his damaged wing hanging down, his head bent, not uttering a sound. Maryan spoke to him but he did not answer. Maryan put his finger to the bird's beak but Stach did not bite. Maryan never saw him eat, drink, or preen, as if he was constantly brooding about the matters that drained away life.

Maryan, too, changed. Until then one never heard of him getting drunk. Now he bought liquor at the tavern, took it home, and drank it. The other fishermen mocked him, saying he was trying to catch fish with nets that had holes in them. Tevya, the night watchman, saw Maryan walking and talking to himself in the middle of the night. Maryan went to the town scribe, Kipa Pevzner, and asked him to write a letter to the warden of the Lublin prison to let him know whether Stach was still there, and, if he had been released, where he could be found. In the middle of dictating the letter, Maryan spat and left.

One Thursday Maryan did not appear in the marketplace. One of the fishermen went to see that happened to him. The shutters were closed. The fisherman knocked but there was no response. He broke the door in and saw Maryan hanging from a hook in the ceiling, an overturned stool at his feet. On his head, clinging to Maryan's hair, was Stach the bird – dead.

Translated by the author

THE LOST WIFE

This story was told to me by a Yiddish writer, not a professional author, but one of those writers who pay to publish their work with a vanity press. When I met him in Buenos Aires, I had never even heard of his existence, but he showed me two published volumes of his poetry. They had even been reviewed locally and in a weekly publication in Mexico or Rio de Janeiro.

He was a tiny man with a bald, grey-fringed skull, and the wrinkled face of a newborn. Though it was a hot summer day, he was wearing a soiled raincoat. He had supported himself as a traveling salesman, he told me, but had developed arthritis and could no longer drag his suitcase. He had, however, managed to keep a few customers who came to him, and so was able to subsist. He lived with a Spanish family on a street in the suburbs. His room had no windows, only a door leading onto a patio, and it was jammed full with books, old newspapers, and all kinds of junk.

He had attached himself to me and for some reason I could not refuse to visit him. To reach his house one had to take three buses. He promised to tell me a fantastic story that he had never before told anyone.

"I would write this story myself if I could write prose," he explained. "But I'm no fiction writer. Some say that I'm no poet either, but that's another matter. On the other hand even if I were a good poet, what difference would it make? Who needs poetry?

Do you smoke? No? You're lucky. The doctor has forbidden me to smoke, but I need it. It's actually my only pleasure other than masturbation.

His final words embarrassed me and I lost patience. "Why are you telling me these things?"

"Why not? When you hear what happened to me you'll understand that I'm not just trying to shock you. Sit down there in that rocking chair. I'll sit on the bed. May I begin?"

"I'm listening."

"Please have a little patience. All these years I've been sure that I would, as the saying goes, take this secret to my grave. First of all, no one cares about me. Secondly, there isn't really any point in my telling it. But when I read your stories I felt that you would understand. Now that you've come here and I've had the honor of meeting you, it's as if it had been destined by heaven.

"I'll begin with my childhood. My father was a poor storekeeper and extremely religious. He was a silent man who seldom spoke to anybody. My mother helped him eke out a living by knitting and sewing for the wealthy. Of their five children three died in infancy. An older sister and I survived. She married early and began to have children. She and the rest of my family perished under the Nazis.

"I once read a tale of yours called 'Shy' and it had a strong impression on me. Shyness is a sickness. The truly shy are capable of doing things that wouldn't even occur to a crazy person. My bashfulness started in childhood and the suffering it caused me is beyond description.

"I had an aunt who lived in a neighboring village and she had a little girl, Hannele. Whenever I heard that my aunt and Hannele were coming to visit I was overcome by such a fit of shyness that I actually became sick. I stopped eating. I couldn't bear the thought that Hannele would see my torn gaberdine, my dirty shirt, my disheveled sidelocks.

"Once when my aunt and cousin spent the night with us I ran away to the outskirts of town and slept in a field. They searched for me all night. When they found me, my father gave me a lashing. He kept yelling, 'Why didn't you come home? Speak up, answer or I'll cripple you.' But I couldn't bring myself to explain that I had done it because I was ashamed before Hannele, since this fact too made me ashamed.

"Shyness is a form of pride, or conversely pride sometimes creates shyness. It's a degrading sickness. Was not shame the punishment for eating of the tree of knowledge? In my opinion many of the world's ills stem from shyness. But let me get on with my story.

"The boys used to go to the ritual bath on Fridays, but I avoided going there as I would the Angel of Death. They used to go swimming in the river in the summertime, too, but it was impossible for me to undress before the others. To this day I suffer from constipation as a result of my bashfulness. I was too shy to go to the outhouse unless no one was around. Sukkes was a torture because it meant eating in the presence of guests. On Simchas Torah, I would steal out of the prayer house before the boys were called up for a group reading of the holy scroll because I was too bashful to stand together with them under the same prayer shawl. In brief, I was too shy to do anything.

"Once on a Purim my father sent me to the house of Baruch Grabover, his good friend, with the traditional gift basket. When I arrived, the house was all lit up, and I saw that the entire family was there – including the women and girls. I was so overcome by shyness that I couldn't go in. What was I to do with the gift? I threw it in the well. A few days passed and my father learned that his friend hadn't received his gift.

"An investigation started, followed by hearings. I was too ashamed to admit that I had thrown such delicacies as an orange, figs, dates and carob beans into a well, and instead confessed that

I had been so tempted that I had eaten them all up. Well, I got it then! I was nicknamed the Purim Glutton and the name stuck until I was grown.

"I could you endless examples, but there's no need.

"Shy people, as you well know, are sometimes amazingly bold. Shy as I was, I was capable of making the most cutting remarks. I became anti-God, anti-Messiah, and blasphemed at an early age. I became an atheist, a Socialist, and what not. I wanted a secular education, and to write Yiddish poetry, though I couldn't even spell properly. For the most part I stayed away from girls, but then suddenly I would behave like a Don Juan. I got a reputation for being arrogant and lecherous.

In short, I played all kinds of roles and complicated my own life. I was daring enough one day to kiss a girl without any warning, and the next would grow red at the mere glimpse of her through a window or the mention of her name. The girls couldn't make heads or tails out of the way that I acted and this actually intrigued them. In addition, my verses were beginning to attract attention. I could have become a ladies man, but possessed as I was by a dybbuk, I never knew what it would drive me to do next. I would arrange a rendezvous and not show up. I would start a love affair, and end it abruptly.

"Today there is such a thing as psychiatry. At that time, it did not exist. And even if it had, I would have preferred being chopped to bitts rather than tell my troubles to anyone.

"Now I'll come to the point. Something happened to the man you see before you that has probably never happened to anyone else. I lost my wife. Not in the sense that she died or ran away with someone else. I literally lost her, as one loses a purse or a watch, and it was all the result of my shyness. Intriguing, isn't it? Don't worry, I'm not going to keep you here all night. Still, I have give you some background, because the story is half crazy as it is, and if I don't fill in a few of the facts, you simply won't believe it.

"There was a girl named Basha in our village and I fell in love with her. To tell the truth, in those days I was always falling in love. Shy people are very romantic. When a man feels that he has little chance with the opposite sex, it makes the challenge that much greater. I fell head over heels in love with Basha. Her father had been a watchmaker. He'd died and her mother had married a man who dealt in hay.

"I had managed to pick up some Hebrew and Basha came to me for Hebrew lessons, but instead of studying grammar, we spent the whole hour talking. It was one of my daring periods. What did she look like? No particularly beautiful. Dark, sort of heavy, with big, black eyes. She had unusually strong, white teeth, and a pretty smile. Basha had an uncle in America to whom she wrote bitter letters. Her stepfather was a coarse man and often insulted her and tormented her mother. He had daughters from a previous marriage and he hadn't been able to marry them off. In short, the household was like a Gehenna. In contrast, our love burned like a flame. There was nothing bashful about *her.*

"I could go on about our affair for three days and nights. Though I loved her, I was ashamed of her. I would never take her out for walks. She took her lesson in a good friend's house. Her friend was a hunchback and because of that I wasn't shy before her. I have many physical defects myself. My shortness is largely to blame for my troubles, although neither of my parents was particularly small. Besides, I don't actually have a neck. My head rests directly on my shoulders. Practically no hair grows on one of my cheeks. I know now that I suffer from an inferiority complex. But that fancy name does not solve my problems.

"Well, Basha wrote to her uncle saying that she would like to come to New York, but that she had a fiancé in Markishov, which is the name of our town, and if her uncle cared about her and wanted to save her life, he would arrange for both of us to come to America.

"At first, her uncle did not reply. Later, his son died in an automobile accident, and he decided to do something for his niece. Letters began to fly back and forth. Finally, her uncle wrote that we should get married and he would send us an affidavit.

"Everything seemed perfect, except that I was too bashful to get married. In our town, a wedding meant a bachelor's party for the groom, being called up to read the holy scroll on the Sabbath, being pelted with raisons and almonds, standing under the canopy, dancing a wedding dance and a whole fuss – and I was too embarrassed to face it all. The mere thought of it made me go hot and cold all over.

"In the meantime, Basha's mother and stepfather had learned the good news, as had my own parents. Everything could have gone off smoothly. We could have been married in Markishov and gone to America. But I schemed and maneuvered so that the wedding would take place in Warsaw. Everyone thought that I had lost my senses.

"Since I was too shy to say that I was too shy to be married at home, I made up all kinds of excuses. I got myself into such a mess that I really almost went crazy. I stopped sleeping. Basha's mother became my mortal enemy. But deceit and sickness wield extraordinary power. I won. Both our parents accompanied us to Warsaw, and there some poor rabbi married us.

"In our town rumor had it that Basha was pregnant. The townspeople didn't know what to think. Truth is often the most incredible thing. Who could have imagined the real reason for our marrying in Warsaw? At times when I am particularly depressed and begin to question God's ways it occurs to me that the answer to everything is undoubtedly a simple one. But since all of Markishov was unable to guess my real motives, why should we humans be able to figure out God's? God might be bashful too.

"Our getting married in Warsaw resulted in a great deal of complications. Basha hadn't grasped the reasons for my actions, either, and she suspected that there was something wrong with me. We were beginning to argue. We spent our wedding night in a hotel, but there was so much noise there that I was unable to consummate our marriage. Now my bashfulness assumed a new form, the fear of impotence. I wanted us to be free of our parents as quickly as possible, and I virtually forced them to go back home. I can say that my shame made me shameless.

"We were alone at last and I finally assured myself that I was a man again. It was time to begin our journey. Our ship was scheduled to leave from Liverpool and we intended to spend a few days in London visiting Basha's cousin, her American uncle's daughter. The trip was an ordeal for me, not because of any discomfort, but because of my shyness. I was ashamed to have my fellow passengers know that Basha and I were married. It seemed to me that people were laughing at us, and perhaps they really were.

"When a person trembles at the thought of being laughed at, he actually becomes laughable. Every minute of that trip to London was fraught with crisis. I constantly felt the urge to throw myself out of the moving train. According to a book I once read by a Freudian, I am homosexual. But I've never felt desire for a man. Still, I suppose that, if you wants to, you can make a case for anything. It's my theory that some people are just too shy to live.

"The journey across the channel was terrible. It stormed and I thought each moment would be my last. The ocean seemed to part like the Red Sea during Exodus and the ship lay almost on its side. Suitcases tumbled across the cabin floor. Everyone was seasick. There were several orthodox Jews on board and they began saying the *Shma*.

"My private hell began once we got to London. My wife's cousin lived in North London in a house where the neighbors were like one big family. Her husband also had flocks of cousins and in-laws and they all came to meet us. They happened to be tall people – almost giants – I looked like a grasshopper among them. In order to take a bath I had to go upstairs and put a penny in a gas meter. I simply couldn't figure it out. The meter did not work properly and Basha's cousin came to help me. I nearly died of embarrassment.

"The first evening they made a party for us. The men wore top hats, the women feathers. They spoke half-English, half-Yiddish. I didn't even understand their Yiddish. They brought presents and joked with me as if the whole thing were one big joke. In the midst of the celebration I got a stomach ache. The toilet was out in the yard and someone showed me the way.

"What happened next I'll never really know. It seems that the courtyard wasn't properly fenced in, and instead of coming back to the right house, I landed in another one. I realized my mistake but could not find my way back, and apparently went even further away. Dogs barked at me. Someone yelled and chased me away, probably thinking that I was a thief. I didn't understand a word of English. When the man ran after me, I ran too.

"After a while it occurred to me that I didn't have my wife's cousin's address with me and that I couldn't remember her married name. I realized that they must have become very anxious back at the house and that they were surely looking for me. The whole situation filled me with such a deep feeling of embarrassment that I raised my eyes to the heavens and said: 'God, do me a favor and take me now.'

"But God dislikes being told what to do. I stood somewhere among buildings that all looked alike, with their funny little chimneys, unable to speak the language and ask directions. I tried to find my cousin's house, but it seems I strayed further and further. Today I know what I should have done. I should have stopped some person, tried to speak to him in Yiddish and, in the worst case, have looked for the police. They would surely have found my relatives. But my shyness made me panic. I was like a three-year-old child, or a sleepwalker.

"London late at night was like a small town, the houses were dark, the streets deserted. I had left my passport behind. I had only my watch and some change.

"Suddenly I saw a park. I sat down on a bench and stayed there like a clay golem, paralyzed by what had happened to me. By that time I no longer even wanted to find my way back. A man who goes to an outhouse and gets lost is ridiculous. It seemed to me that there was more honor in a mysterious disappearance than in the return of a *shlemiel.* I decided to vanish. Rather than be a fool in a farce, I'd be the hero of a tragedy. It is clear to me now that I simply ran away like Jonah fled from God.

"I sat in the park until daybreak. It was summertime and the weather wasn't bad. It began to rain but it soon stopped. There was lightening without thunder. I had read in religious books about the war between the Angel of Good and the Angel of Evil. That minute I felt clearly within me the struggle between these two powers. The Good Angel spoke: 'What is happening to you? From whom are you running away? And why? In the morning, go out into the street, tell whomever you meet what has happened, and you will be helped. Your shame is a sickness and a mortal sin. It will lead you to the abyss.'

"But something in me – something stubborn, proud, fatalistic – argued. 'You've already been disgraced. The family is laughing at you. Basha has already lost all respect for you.'

"I no longer had any real desire either for Basha or to go to America. I was also convinced that from then on I would be impotent. Can anyone explain insanity? Dawn came and the sun rose, red as blood. I wished I were dead. But to kill oneself one also needs courage. When day came I had come to a decision: I would remain hidden and never show my face in the house where I had disgraced myself.

"Early that morning I passed a small synagogue. I walked inside and found several Jews praying. A beadle brought me a prayer book, phylacteries, and a prayer shawl. I told him that I was a bachelor and he took back the prayer shawl. I prayed along with the others, though I was not a believer. They were all in a hurry. They left out entire passages. They must have been salesmen or artisans anxious to get to work. They finished praying and left.

"The beadle came up to me and asked who I was and where I lived. I wanted to tell him what had happened to me but I couldn't. Instead I told him that I had just come to London and been unable to find work. 'Where do you live?' he asked again, and I replied, 'In the street.'

"Your story doesn't sound right to me, he said, but I'm not one to stick my nose into someone else's business. You've deserted you wife, haven't you?

"Yes," I said.

"Then why don't you say so?"

He told me that he had had a shrew for a wife and that he had barely managed to free himself from her. He knew a man who needed a worker and promised to take me to him and said I could lodge at his place for two shillings a week.

I decided that my disappearance would be reported in the newspaper and that the police would be looking for me. But I had by now made up my mind that if they found me I would refuse to go back to my wife. I had but one wish – not to be laughed at. If I were caught, I decided to say that that I had deserted my wife. Let them put me in jail. Let them deport me to Poland. I feared nothing except going back to my wife's cousin's house and facing the questions and ridicule that awaited me there.

"The beadle lived in a half-ruin and he took me to a man who owned a doll factory. He employed a few women who spoke to each other in Italian. I did all kinds of menial work: swept up, scrubbed the floor, pasted labels on boxes. I was paid a pound a week. The women laughed at me. I could not speak to them since they knew only English and Italian. I walked around like a dummy. The boss told me what to do in Yiddish.

"The whole factory consisted of one room. There was a terrible stench, and the dust choked me. Yet in my perverted mind anything seemed better than to return to a wife whom I loved and who loved me. These are the facts.

"I was consistently afraid of being discovered. Who might know? Had my picture appeared in the newspapers? Were the police looking for me? I was like a fugitive. But apparently the factory women didn't read the papers and Scotland Yard was busy looking for bigger fish. I remained in the country illegally and no one bothered me. I went from the beadle's house to the factory and from the factory back to the beadle's house. The beadle did his own cooking and he fixed my meals as well. He was a strange little man – boorish, half savage. He came from Galicia. For some reason or other he had become a deadly enemy of the female sex. He claimed that all women were adulteresses and evil. The fact that I had deserted my wife improved his opinion of me. Don't ask me how filthy the place was! He lived like an animal. Oddly enough, he had almost forgotten Yiddish, though he hadn't learned another language. He mixed all his languages together – Yiddish, Polish, Ukrainian, English – and mutilated them all. In addition to being a beadle he had another job, but I don't remember what it was.

"Never in my life have I met a more primitive person. He was short, husky, with red cheeks and a patchy yellowish beard – a clump here, a clump there. He was like a Neanderthal Man living in the twentieth century. At times, when I didn't understand his gibberish, he would fall into a rage. He had wide, yellow teeth so strong that he could crack peach pits. How he had managed to get to London, heaven only knows.

"The day came and passed when my wife and I had been scheduled to leave for America. At first, each day seemed like a year. My thoughts almost drove me crazy. Later, I became as numb as the beadle with whom I lived.

"There are tragedies that make people greater and those that leave them hardened and dumb. What happened to me, and the way in which I reacted, made me lose my self-respect, and once that happens, you stop being a person. I stopped thinking altogether and lived in a state of lethargy. Still, my work improved, and my boss raised my pay a few shillings. I had only one wish – to have a room of my own. But this was too much of a luxury. During all that time, I hadn't written a single letter home because I had been too ashamed of what had happened, and my parents had assumed that I was dead. I later learned that my father had even wanted to observe the traditional week of mourning for me.

"What happened after that It's not important. Or perhaps it is. By chance I met some missionaries with whom I made friends. I did this mainly because I hoped that in the event I was arrested, they could help me.

"The business with the missionaries is a chapter in itself. They were led by a converted Jew, a former preacher to whom a woman, also a missionary, had attached herself. She had a beard and was passionately in love with him. But he didn't want to marry her. The whole thing wasn't clear to me then and still isn't after all these years. Millions of books have been created from the letters of the alphabet. Imagine the numberless situations to be pieced together out of human emotions and circumstances. You never know what you may stumble on. This woman was both crazy and cunning, religious and promiscuous, and though she prattled about Jesus day and night, she observed all the Jewish holidays and even used the Hebrew prayer-book. She was the daughter of a Rabbi.

"I could tell you how I got from England to Argentina, and about my life here. But that is not relevant. The fact is that I never remarried. I have never touched another woman, not even a prostitute. I did eventually write to my parents, but by then my father was dead. He died believing that I was already in the world to come. I heard from my mother that my wife had married her American uncle and had had several children by him. Later, the uncle died and she went to live in Canada.

"The important thing is that, all these years, I have remained alone. I failed, and I have never been able to gather the courage to try again. Lately even my shyness has disappeared. I wanted to become a poet, but the critics didn't like my work, and there's nothing one can do about that.

"One thing I have learned through the years and that is not to feel resentful toward anyone. There are reasons for everything, and even the reasons have reasons. A man's character is his fate. My mother used to say: What you takes out of the cradle, you put back in the grave.

Translated by Joseph Singer

THE PASS

On the bed lay a small man, stark naked, with a little black beard and gray in the middle. His high sunburned forehead was pink and peeling. A beak-like nose, marked by a pince-nez, projected from between two round bird-like eyes. His false teeth rested on the night table beside a book bearing the title *Spirit and Reality*. Professor Javitz scratched his hairy chest and from time to time glanced absently at his forearm. "God, so much hair," he thought aloud, then, "Darwin was certainly right." The beads of perspiration forming on the professor's forehead clung to the dead skin. The air conditioning in his Miami hotel room was not functioning though he had put in a complaint to room service several hours before. There was nothing further he could do. Meanwhile the thermometer registered a sweltering 98 degrees, and the professor shifted uncomfortably in the wet bedclothes.

"I've certainly committed a folly. What nonsense to have come to Miami in the summer. As if it weren't hot enough in New York. How could I have been taken in by foolish advertisements? Well, it's done. I'll have to bear it for another five days. I'll imagine that I'm in a hospital or a prison. Suppose I were in Russia, accused of left-wing or right-wing deviation. God in heaven! How close I came to being there. They'd already stamped the visa on my passport." Professor Javitz smiled. With the palm of his hand he mopped the wet turf of hair that remained in the middle of his head. "Yes, one makes mistakes. The last thing which a man does in his life is probably a mistake. "The Logic of Mistakes" – have I seen a book like that or is it my own idea? Suppose that to the geometry of Lobachevsky and Riemann one added a geometry built on false conclusions. The trouble is that the number of false geometries would be infinite. They may well try that too. 'A' is not 'A.' My own life might be called false mathematics: false axioms, false definitions, false conclusions. What was my coming here in the middle of August if not an erroneous calculation?

"And how about Esther? What would happen if I phoned her now? After two and a half years of silence, suddenly, 'Hello, it's me, David.' Assuming that she still lives there, that she hasn't married, that she's at home now and that she'd be willing to talk to me – what would I say to her? Well, I'm not going to do it anyhow. Inertia can increase no less than momentum. A new Newtonian formula: the longer a spirit is at rest, the greater the force necessary to set it in motion. The question is, why did I ever stop calling her? What if I had to explain it to somebody? Say, in a courtroom. We had everything – love, sex, comraderie. Suddenly I stopped calling her. Why, why? Could I formulate it? Yes. I became a hypochondriac and had the illusion that she wanted to destroy me, spiritually, with thoughts, words, a modern kind of incantation. I actually fled from murder by magic like someone who believes in Voodoo. I was afraid of the evil eye or some such superstition. She spoke too much about death. Even in bed. She'd fallen into necromancy. Would a writer be able to do justice to such a situation? No, it wouldn't sound real. The result would be farfetched, a melodramatic piece of literature. But that kind of melodrama has actually stopped an old love and has left me a lonesome man. Would anybody believe that I, a rationalist, could have succumbed to mysticism? And why didn't she ever call? Is it possible that she divined what I was running away from? Perhaps her brain worked in quite a different way. Would a Dostoevsky or a Proust be able to describe such a state of affairs? No, no writer can set down the real truth. It's too irrational, too fantastic, too insane. The truth, like a nightmare, can never be told."

Professor Javits turned his face to the wall. "I'm tired. Perhaps I'll be able to sleep." He shoved the wet pillow off the bed. For a while his mind was at rest. Then he began to think about his savings. In thirty years he had saved barely eight thousand dollars. What if he should lose his job? Assuming that death would not overtake him for twenty more years, what would he do? Yes, social security. He would seek out the cheapest island on the globe and settle there. He would read, eat, sleep. Boring? It couldn't be more boring than New York. He would depend on fishing to supply him with food. When one fished for sustenance, it was perhaps more interesting. What would he read? Not philosophy or literature, to be sure. He'd study mathematics, physics, chemistry. Perhaps he would keep an island woman, as Gauguin had done. The main thing would be, naturally, not to come down with cancer or a heart attack before then.

Suddenly the tedious Miami vacation was over and Professor Javitz was back in New York. He was no longer hot but he was still naked. He found himself not in his own apartment, but in a strange flat, large and bare, opening on a long corridor. On a table rested a telephone. He tried to call Esther, but in vain. The telephone dial behaved in a strange way, turning round and round. Perhaps a screw was loose or something. He tried to call the operator. No answer. Not even a dial tone. "Maybe the wire isn't connected. Maybe there's no electricity here at all. Why didn't I make sure before I signed the lease? And why is the fire escape on the inside? How would one get out in case of a fire? Unless everything is made of asbestos. I must see the superintendent." He wanted to dress but his clothes were nowhere in sight. He opened the wardrobe. A skirt was hanging from a hook. "What's a skirt doing here? I'm not a woman. Or perhaps they took me for a Scot?" He had to call somebody – a neighbor, a janitor, anybody. He opened the outside door but instead of the hall he faced a long drop. He looked down into an unknown depth, an abyss. The house seemed to have been sliced with a huge knife or an atomic bomb. The foundations of the building were not to be seen. He clutched the doorknob and tried to plant his feet firmly on the threshold. Professor Javitz was confused. "Let's assume that the house was split, but why is there no light? Or has the H-bomb divided the earth into halves, with one of the halves turning away from the sun?" He was looking into those very depths which geologists never hoped to see. The core of the earth lay bare. "It most probably consists of gold. But in a cosmic catastrophe like this, what value does gold have? And how could it be mined? The ladder would have to be four thousand miles long. Where could I get so much rope, wire, and wood? Unless I could borrow Jacob's ladder …"

Professor Javitz laughed. He wanted to retreat but, turning back, he found that his apartment had begun to sink. It hinged on a beam or a log. He was standing between two abysses. He still clutched the knob for dear life. The door itself seemed to hang on nothing. "How does gravitation work here?" Professor Javitz wondered. "Some point of support must exist." He became panicked. What should he do? How long could he exist that way? He wanted to cry for help but who was there to help him? The stairs below had disappeared. He was hovering over an unfathomable darkness. He wasn't even sure if the physical laws were still valid here. He might already be in a different sphere, in a fourth dimension. Perhaps the laws of nature here were based on Einstein and Cantor. This was the limit of all limits. There wasn't even any air here. He began to choke.

He felt a pressure on his heart, a heaviness, as if a bulldozer were crushing him, a mortifying pressure. There was a crisp brittle sound. Something snapped, broke. It was the end, the end.

The earthly heaviness was lifted, leaving a gap and complete darkness. He was suspended in space. A thread connected him to some substance. At once Esther was near him. He didn't see her but he felt her presence.

"How did you manage to get here?"

"I just managed."

"Why didn't you ever call?"

"How? I couldn't."

"Did you get married or something?"

"Of course not."

"What have you done?"

"I waited for you."

"Did you guess why I stopped calling?"

"Yes, yes my dear."

They embraced and kissed. He was kissing her slowly and wondering why he wasn't breathless. He spoke without a voice, without words.

"How long does this last?" he asked.

"It's one long orgasm."

For a long while he was listening and silent, with a kind of silence which he'd never experienced before. Presently he understood.

"Why did you do it? When?" he asked.

"About a year ago."

"How? Why?"

"Oh, it was all so easy. You left and you stopped calling. I was literally bored to death."

"Why didn't *you* call?"

"You know me."

"Tell me the truth. You wanted me to die that time."

"Yes, darling."

"Why? Why?"

"Because I wanted to have all of you."

"So I wasn't mistaken."

"No, my love. There are no mistakes."

"I'm still connected by some thread. Or what is it?"

"Yes, it's the last connection with your body."

"Where is it? Do you see it? I'm completely blind."

"You only imagine so. You'll get accustomed. You're like a newly hatched chick."

For a long while both were silent. They neither stood nor lay but soared diagonally up, lightly and rhythmically, like a pair of birds. The darkness dissolved but it was not replaced by light. In the dusk he saw two mountains, their summits lost in a cloud. They had reached a boundary. They circled above it like airplanes which cannot land.

"Where will we stay?"

"There where we are."

"What will we do?"

She laughed and he laughed with her, both voiceless. There were no more questions, no more riddles. All inhibitions, all doubts, were gone. Time and space vanished and with them the categories of reason. Here was everything: pure love, perfect sex, infinite unity.

"Do you see your body already?"

"Not yet."

"Somebody's taking your wallet. What's that? Oh, your travelers checks."

Both laughed again. How quickly it had all happened! He no longer needed a telephone to call Esther. She was with him to stay. And he'd planned on twenty years more of that misery! At that very moment they crossed the pass between the mountains: the gateway to eternity.

Translated by Martha Glicklich

FATAL

It was one of those loves that novelists call "fatal." We met in Warsaw at a gathering of people who called themselves "The Schnorers." Most of them worked in stores and banks, and they all had an interest in the arts. One young man sang Yiddish folk songs. A young woman quoted Slowacski and Bialik. An amateur artist had painted a cubist portrait of Mrs. Glick, the host. Her husband, Mendel Glick, was a bookkeeper, and he read an ode he'd written for Mrs. Glick's birthday. Mendal and I had been at *Heder* together on Twarda Street. For years we had been out of contact. Then he read a sketch of mine in *The Epoch* and looked me up. I remembered him as a gentle boy. His nickname was The Little Mezuzah. But he had grown up to be a broad shouldered giant with a deep voice.

Mendel had bought twenty copies of *The Epoch* and sent them to his friends. At the party, I was like a famous man. A young woman named Lola came up to me and said, "I read your sketch. You understand women." As she gave me her hand – small, boney, strong – I knew that something was starting between us. She was slim, not tall, with a thin waist, a flat bosom and the muscular legs of a dancer. She had bobbed black hair. Her face was light, pointed, with sunken cheeks, eyes that were a mix of green and brown, and boyish ears. She wore a black velvet skirt and a white blouse embroidered in red. Someone told me that she had danced, written poems, and been one of the best fashion designers in Warsaw. She had her own shop and wealthy women wore her clothes.

After a while she began to read her poems, which were written in Polish. She tried to imitate Alexander Bloch, Mayakovsky, and other Russian modernists – or "futurists," as we called them in Warsaw. She even used "obscene" language.

I criticized her poem, which she called "The Worm," and she said to me, "You may be right, but you're mean just the same."

I'd never seen a woman drink so much. Lola drank one glass of vodka after another. Between glasses, she smoked cigarettes through an amber holder. She got drunk and began to dance, singing *Ochy Chernye*, mimicking the music hall singers. She came over to me and said, "I guess my poetry is as bad as my marriage. I spit on everything, including God."

I had had a few drinks too, and with a daring that was out of character I asked, "Are you married at the moment?"

"Why do you want to know? Are you trying to start up with me?"

"Maybe."

"Men get burned by me. They curse the day they met me."

"What's the date today?" I asked. I took out a notebook and wrote it down.

"Since you're already scribbling," she said, "take down my address and telephone number."

Later, Mendel told me about her. Her father was a Talmudic scholar, a disciple of the Gur Rabbe. He'd died of typhoid during the German occupation. Lola's sister had lived with a Czarist officer who, after the Russian Revolution, had become a taxi driver in Berlin. Her mother, who was paralyzed, lived with her. I had thought she was about twenty-five, but Mendel told me that she was over thirty and had already had two husbands.

"Be careful with her," he warned me. "She's a wild beast."

"What's she done?"

"Plenty. She even tried to hang herself."

When I finally told Mendel that I was about to go home, Lola said, "Let's go together."

It was dark on the steps. We stopped on the second floor and kissed for a long time. Her mouth smelled of liquor and chocolate. She asked, "Do you have a wife?"

"No."

"A lover?"

"No," I lied.

"I'm a loose woman, but I hate to share."

We waited at the gate for a long time before the janitor let us out. Outside, I hailed a droshky. Lola lived on Solna Street. While riding we held hands and she told me about her past. She's finished the gymnasium but couldn't afford to go to university. She'd fallen in love with her literature teacher and they were about to get married when she found out that he had converted to Christianity. She wouldn't have minded, but her mother would have died of grief. He soon comforted himself with a rich widow. On Leszno, Lola told me quite openly that I could stay the night with her. At the Writers Club I often heard stories about meeting a woman and going to bed with her on the first night, but I always considered it boasting. My own affairs always started slowly and went on and on with interruptions, postponements, long walks, and a lot of talking. The real affair always came after a quarrel and after I had already given up all hope. Suddenly I was sitting in a droshky going home with a woman I had only known a few hours. I trembled with fear and desire. Lola smoked one cigarette after another and pressed her knee against mine.

"How long has it been since you broke up with your girl?" she asked me.

I wanted to say three months, but I said, "three weeks."

"It doesn't take you very long to go from one to another," she said. "In that case, let's just be friends. We'll have tea and then you'll go home. I hate men for their treachery, but I hate women even more. I thank God I'm a female myself and don't have to deal with these creatures. I pity men because they have to put up with these false selfish monsters. Don't think I consider myself an exception. When I read your story I thought: this man understands us. And I wanted to get to know you."

We walked up two flights of steps and down a long corridor. Lola took me into a room full of mirrors. There was a sewing mannequin in the corner. When I went into the toilet I could hear groaning from across the hall. It was her mother complaining to Lola, possibly about her conduct. I was ashamed of myself. I began to think about Lola's two husbands. She must have had about two dozen lovers too. What was so great about getting entangled with a woman like this? I remembered my father's words: "The Evil One does not deal in bargains. He sells you dirt, and you pay in gold."

It didn't take me long to see all of Lola's flaws. She was hysterical and went to doctors for her nerves. She couldn't sleep without pills. She drank too much, smoked three packs of cigarettes a day, and fought with the girls who worked for her. When her mother reproached her, Lola insulted her and threatened to hit her. But everybody said the same thing: she was excellent at her work. She could see the most elaborate dress in a shop window and immediately go home and copy it. She also designed her own patterns. Although she was a first class tailor, her prices were reasonable and she had a lot of customers. She ate very little – sometimes nothing more than a roll and sausage all day. When there was a lot of work, she could sit all night at the sewing machine drinking one cup of black coffee after another, filling several ashtrays with butts and ashes. I once heard her mother tell her that she was killing herself, and Lola replied, "So? There'll be one less piece of garbage."

Everyday I swore to end our relationship. Lola was already accusing me out of jealousy. She sent her friends to spy on me. When I told her I was going home, she called me every half hour. If I said I was going to the Writers Club, she phoned me there. When she caught me lying, she made scenes. I resented her tactics and also thought about her past. Men kept calling her. She spoke to them like good friends and, from the way she responded, I could tell that they showed little respect for her. In bed she swore me eternal love but in sober moments I knew we couldn't last. My idea of a wife was someone like my mother: modest and devoted. When Lola got me to admit this, she called me a hypocrite. I deceived her and trembled at the thought that she was deceiving me. But my desire for her grew just the same. If we quarreled, I lay awake at night, and Lola admitted that she did too. My work began to suffer. I couldn't keep to any schedules. I started a novel and got stuck in the middle. Lola was about to be granted a divorce from her second husband and she asked me to tell her definitively whether I was ready to marry her or not. I gave her a definitive answer: "No."

"In that case, it's all over. Get out!"

But moment I got back to my room and opened the door the telephone rang. Lola screamed and cursed like a market woman. One of her friends called me from outside the shop to tell me that she was breaking dishes and tearing up dresses in her rage. We made peace, but a few days later a new argument broke out. It was fortunate that her husband dragged out the divorce. He wanted money and was trying to persuade her to come back to him. He worked in a dry goods store on Gesia Street and I went to see what he looked like. He was a huge man with a head of curly hair, like a ram, and a nose to match. He joked with his employer, cursed, and flashed his gold teeth. The idea that Lola had lived with this brute made me queasy.

Outside I lifted my arms to heaven and swore again by God, by my parents, and by my own soul to run from her as from the plague.

Weeks passed, months, a year or two, but the quarrels, peace-making, and reproaches never stopped. Everyday there was a new crisis. I went to Zakopane for vacation. Lola was in the middle of her busiest season so she couldn't travel. The moment I arrived in the mountain town, I received a telegram from her saying that her mother had died. Lola's behavior at the funeral and later at the cemetery shocked and shamed me. She scratched her face with her nails and called herself a murderess. She tried to throw herself into the grave and had to be dragged away. After her mother's death, her business began to fall apart. She drank more and worked less. Her friends abandoned her one after the other. She wasn't earning enough for her daily expenses and asked me for money. She was behind with the rent. Her phone was shut off. In the morning she didn't make her bed and walked around sleepily with disheveled hair, a torn housecoat, and old broken slippers. Every night she dreamed that her mother berated her and pinched her. Lola showed me the bruises on her arms and breast. She went to a doctor who told her she was being poisoned by nicotine. I was with her at the doctor's office and I heard her say, "I'll still smoke – even in hell."

As Lola's situation worsened, mine became better. Sketches of mine appeared in the newspapers and I had published a book that got good reviews. I finally got my own little apartment.

One evening Lola came to see me unexpectedly and found a girl reading poems to me. Her name was Etel Schnitzer. She was tall and bulky, with a big chest and broad hips. Her poetry was too delicate for her looks. She had a thick nose and fleshy lips. I had put out a plate of cookies and she had eaten them all. I had closed my eyes and heard her reading with a lisp, as if her tongue was too big for her mouth:

> Oh, Sun, how can you shine
> When my tender heart is full
> Of eternal darkness!

Suddenly Lola burst in drunk. She carried a basket with a nightshirt and some cosmetics. "Who is this whore?" she screamed.

She ran over to the girl, spat at her, ripped the manuscript from her hands and tore it up. In her rage she turned over chairs, threw my books on the floor, and cursed in Yiddish, Polish, and Russian. The girl took what was left of her poems and ran out. I grabbed Lola's hands. She shrieked violently and fought with a strength that astonished me. In her haste to get out, Etel Schnitzer had left the first page of her manuscript, which had her address on it. Lola saw it and hollered, "Now I know where she lives. Tomorrow I'll leave her cold."

"Lola, I swear by everything that is holy to me that I haven't even touched her."

"The angel of death will touch her. I'll tear her apart, limb by limb. There'll be nothing left to bury. Murderer! Whoremonger! Outcast!"

This wasn't the usual jealous scene: it was an outburst of insanity. Lola tried to break my furniture and destroy my papers by pouring ink on them. She spat, hissed, bit, and kicked. She tried to jump out of the window. I had to knock her out, and I hit her so hard I became frightened. I dragged her over to the door and tried to throw her out, but her legs gripped mine with astounding force. She raved, coughed, choked and foamed at the mouth like an epileptic. She gasped, "I'll stab her! Her filthy blood will run all over the gutters! Thug, pimp, bastard!" After wrangling for what felt like hours we both collapsed – I on the sofa, she on the floor. At dawn I fell asleep and Lola waked me. She growled, "Take me for the last time."

"Why the last?" I asked bewildered.

"Because tomorrow I'm going to finish off Etel Schnitzer."

I turned on the lamp and saw that Lola had two black eyes. There was dried blood on her swollen lips. Her face was white as a corpse.

In Paris, a new Yiddish paper was being formed and the editor, a friend of mine from Warsaw, invited me to work for it. I saw this as an act of providence. The French consul gave me a visa and my Polish passport came through without delay. I packed a suit, some shirts, my manuscripts, and went to Paris. I arrived on a rainy morning and the taxi took me to a one-star hotel in Belleville. Saying goodbye to Lola would have ended in chaos.

I worked as a journalist for the newspaper and in my free hours I tried to do some writing for myself. I studied French and frequented the Yiddish writers' café. They spoke a lot about Yiddish literature but it was pointless: there was neither a publisher in Paris nor enough Yiddish readers. The younger generation had been brought up on French. The older people were mostly interested in leftist politics.

I wrote Lola one letter without giving my address. I got acquainted with a woman painter, Mina Vishover, fifteen years older than I was. Mina suffered from paranoia. She wouldn't allow Chagall's name to be mentioned in her presence. Any time she heard his name, she'd turn pale and say all kins of terrible things about him. She called him a fake and accused him of hypnotizing the critics. Mina had been divorced from an engineer whom she accused of trying to poison her. We lived in neighboring rooms at the hotel. Her room was also her studio. It smelled of oil paint and turpentine. Strangely enough, though she attacked Chagall, she tried to imitate fantastic animals and small-town Jews with wings, horns, and tails. Her bed was always piled with canvasses, papers, brushes. Mina smoked in bed and burned holes in the blanket. Even though she was small, wrinkled, and bowlegged, she boasted that men chased after her. She thought that all the great painters copied her and that the art dealers robbed her.

Meanwhile the newspaper I worked for couldn't withstand the competition of the Yiddish communist press and closed down. The publisher owed me a few hundred francs. I was having difficulties prolonging my visa. Mina had a relative in London and went to visit her for a week, but a month passed and she didn't return. Somehow I managed to scrape together travel expenses and return to Warsaw.

I tried to call Lola but her phone had been cut off. I went to stay the night with a friend. The Warsaw magazine that had published my sketches had folded. At the Writer's Club I applied for a loan. The secretary, a modernistic poet and a translator of Gottfried Benn, told me that there was no money in the treasury and that, besides, the board that decided on the loans wouldn't meet for two weeks. I asked him if he knew a poetess by the name of Etel Schnitzer.

"She's a bad penny."

"I heard somewhere that she had some misfortune," I said.

"What kind of misfortune? Every time she writes a poem it's a misfortune."

I made a holy oath not to look for Lola and not to begin the misery anew. I had no apartment, no girlfriend. Furnished rooms had become extremely expensive. I had an address book with telephone numbers, but every woman I called had a different excuse. Some were engaged, some had gotten married. One had become a teacher in the provinces. One woman hung up when she heard my voice, angry because I never wrote her.

Every day I climbed scores of steps and rang innumerable doors. Dogs barked at me. I was shown rooms with peeling walls smelling of bedbugs and insect repellant. One woman asked me what my profession was. When I told her I was a Yiddish writer, she said, "And from this you make a living?" She told me that she had a brother-in-law who wrote Yiddish plays and that his wife supported him. In another apartment the door was opened by a round little woman with red cheeks and a blond wig. She showed me a room so tiny it could hardly contain a bed. The price was reasonable and I was about to give a deposit but after some hesitation the woman said, "I'd like to ask you something but don't be angry."

"What do you want to ask?"

"Do you ever have women in your room?"

"It might happen."

"In that case I can't rent it to you."

"What do you care?" I asked.

She blushed, smiled good naturally and sheepishly, "I get jealous."

Late in the evening I happened to cross Solna Street. My feet seemed to lead me there. The gate to Lola's building was still open. I went up the dark steps, calling myself a wretch and an idiot. I tried to ring the bell but the buzzer was missing. I pushed the latch and the door opened. The corridor was dark. Was the apartment empty? Was Lola already asleep? I was sure that if I found her at home it would be with a lover. My going there was crazy, but wasn't my whole situation crazy?

I quietly opened the door to her bedroom. I heard double breathing. I approached the bed on my tiptoes. A gas lamp shone through the window and my eyes got used to the darkness. Lola was sleeping with someone, but it was not a man. It was a woman whose long hair hung to her shoulders. I looked closer and recognized Etel Schnitzer. Lola wore a pair of tailored pajamas. Etel had a lace nightgown. They seemed to me like two dolls but both of them snored. Lola sighed in her sleep. She appeared to have aged during our separation. Her eyebrows had become thick. She smiled in a mannish way that seemed unfamiliar.

I stood there gaping, holding my breath. I didn't know what was stronger in me – my curiosity or my feeling of loss. After a while I left. In the corridor I stumbled against a chair and banged my knee. I gave the janitor ten groschen and he opened the gate. I knew I wouldn't sleep that night. I walked to the Vienna Station, sat down on a bench, and stayed there until daybreak.

Translated by the author and Laurie Colwin

THE PROFESSOR'S WIFE

I met her on a bus riding down a narrow winding road somewhere in Italy, I think between Sorrento and Naples, or perhaps between Amalfi and Sorrento. I had slept badly the night before and the morning was foggy and cool.

It was a small bus, its seats, with torn upholstery, were almost empty. If I'm not mistaken, the American woman and I were the only passengers. I sat to the right of the driver and she to the left. She continually asked him questions about the sea, about the hills, the villas, and many other questions, as one sometimes hears with children whose curiosity can never be satisfied. Her voice was also like a little girl's. The driver spoke a broken English and I could see he had great difficulty answering her. The road seemed to me quite dangerous. With the slightest mistake we could have fallen from a great height right into the Mediterranean. I had an urge to tell the lady to leave the driver in peace if she intended to arrive where she was going. Just the same, I kept silent.

The woman was in her early thirties. Her face was ruined from acne. I noticed that she bit her nails and that her fingers had ink spots, like that of a schoolgirl. Her dress was also on the sloppy side, like a teenager's. Her ash blonde hair was held together with a rubber band. After a while she began to talk to me, even though we had not been introduced: where do I come from, where was I going, what was my profession, am I married. I answered all her questions with the tone of a sedate man who tolerates the chattering of an *enfant terrible*. After a while I asked her without standing on ceremony: How about you? Where do you come from, where are you going?

"I'm from Chicago. My husband is a professor. We were supposed to go to Europe together but at the last moment he changed his mind. He dug up some conference or God-knows-what. He had to present a paper. So we decided that I would go by myself. Until about a week and a half ago I was receiving mail from him every day and sometimes even a few letters in the same day. He knew my travel plan and all the addresses. Wherever I came the hotel clerk gave me some mail. Suddenly he went silent. I've cabled him a few times and tried to talk to him on the telephone, but there's no answer. I'm going absolutely crazy."

"Maybe he's traveling too?"

"No. He was supposed to stay in the city. Even if he was traveling, he could still write to me. I'm not sleeping nights. Sometimes I imagine that he's lying dead in our apartment. It's summer and all of our friends have left the city. He could have died not once but ten times and no one would give a hoot."

"Don't you have any relatives in Chicago?"

"No relatives. What do you think I should do?"

"You have to decide for yourself."

"I thought of going back but my ship is leaving Naples in three weeks. I'm a coward. I don't fly. I'm absolutely in despair. May I sit down near you?"

"Of course."

"Come. Let's sit farther back. We're disturbing the driver. I'm sick and tired of all this beautiful scenery. More palms, and more flowers. It's gorgeous, it's magnificent, but there is a deadness to it all. If he was here, I'd enjoy each minute. Alone it's all a big drag.

I don't know Yiddish, but my grandmother read the newspaper you write for. As children she'd read us, what do you call them, those letters from the reader, and it was terribly interesting."

"What does your husband teach?"

"Mathematics. I was never good at mathematics. I got the worst grades. To this day I don't have the slightest clue what its all about, but he's a wiz at it. Calculus, analytical geometry, who knows what else. I envy the wives whose husbands teach literature. These women can speak to their men about the subject they teach. I can't say anything to him about mathematics except that I hate it."

"Don't you have any children?"

"Children, no. What for? Who wants to bother with a little boy who screams all day and makes a slave out of you. What satisfaction can this give? Absolutely none. Irving would have liked to have a baby, but I told him: not with me. You get nothing out of them when they're small and you know how little gratitude they show when they grow up. As long as I can, I want to enjoy my life. I just had an idea. It'd be good if we could have children in old age. Let's say that a woman would begin to get pregnant and give birth at sixty or even at seventy. Isn't that a good idea?"

"Tell it to God."

"Is there a God? Look how he's driving. It'll be a miracle if we get there alive."

Strangely, we'd both made reservations at the same hotel. Not that there was a big choice. We actually became neighbors. We ate supper together in the half-empty dining room, a large Italian meal with plates of fruit as dessert. The professor's wife – I call her that because I've forgotten her name – asked for a paper bag and packed in it some apples, oranges, and grapes which she took to her room.

I forgot to mention that the moment we entered the hotel she immediately asked if there was any mail for her. The answer was none. For a while she seemed disturbed, she gave me a worried look, but it lasted only a minute. She soon recollected herself.

After the meal, a long silence ensued. She looked at me as if she were asking what we should do now. There was a time when I dreamed of such adventures – a trip abroad, another man's wife. But only a few weeks before I'd written an article where I said that the Ten Commandments are not only divine laws but also the very principles of civilization and those who defy them become immediately part of the underworld. Thou shall not kill and thou shall not commit adultery are two sides of one coin. I compared a man who has dealings with another man's wife to a Nazi. I did not now intend to turn all this into a joke because of this female whose husband may be lying sick and helpless in his apartment in Chicago. Who knows? His tortured soul may be hovering right here in this darkly lit dining room, watching and waiting to see our next move. If we behaved badly this soul may quote my article before the throne of glory and denounce me saying: 'see, Father in heaven, what he preaches, and how he conducts himself.' On the other hand, if the professor was dead, this would no longer be adultery. The professor's wife suddenly asked:

"What do you think has happened?"

"I don't know. There are many possibilities."

"What possibilities?"

"Perhaps he's fallen in love with someone else."

"Even so, he wouldn't remain silent. I always told him, if you don't love me anymore, tell me openly and clearly. I want you to know that my husband is not some light-minded young man. He's twenty years older than I am. He's not the type to run around with women."

"Perhaps he's in the hospital, God forbid."

"If he was conscious, he'd send word. But as far as I know, he's quite healthy. But who can tell?"

We soon went upstairs to our floor and for a while we stood between her door and my door. The professor's wife hesitated for a while. "Would you like to come to my room?" she said.

I heard myself answer, "Perhaps a little later."

"Very well. Come later. This place is empty and boring."

I entered my room and was immediately at a loss as what to do with myself. I had nothing to read and neither did I have any desire to write. From the window I could see a courtyard where many barrels were standing. My thoughts returned to the professor. I could see him lying in the middle of a room, a body in the process of decay, with a yellow face and with one eye half opened. He most probably cried for help when he got the heart attack. Perhaps he tried to call someone on the telephone but fell down knowing it was his end. He most probably thought about his young wife, whom he let go to Europe by herself.

I knew in advance what would happen if I visited her room. We would babble for a while until we fell upon one another. If there is a God, He would look upon us with his divine eyes and think, "Miserable hypocrite! You don't fool me. I know how to deal with scoundrels like you."

I wasn't as afraid of His punishment as I was ashamed of Him. This is the same God to whom I pray whenever I'm in trouble, and from whom I demand that he should avenge the Nazis for that they did to the Jews. How can I myself behave like a Nazi? I decided firmly not to go visit the professor's wife. I laid down on the bed in my clothes and after a while I began to doze. I awoke to someone knocking at my door. I had forgotten where I was. I called out: "Who's there?"

"It's me, your neighbor. You were supposed to visit me. Were you asleep? I'm sorry."

It became quiet. She must have gone back to her room. After a while I got up and opened the door and no one was there. I had missed out on a little play with this frivolous creature. But I'd convinced myself that I was not completely without character, that what I said and wrote had some weight.

The next morning when I went down to breakfast she was gone. She'd left without saying goodbye. I imagined that the evil spirit was saying to me, "There is no God and the powers that *do* exist care little who sleeps with whom. It's all nonsense, unnecessary guilt, cowardice, irrational fear."

"If these powers don't care who sleeps with whom," I answered the Evil One, "they should also be indifferent to who steals from whom, and who kills whom. And in that case, the Nazis have done nothing wrong."

"They did wrong from a human point of view, not from a cosmic point of view," the Evil One replied. "Don't people treat animals the way the Nazis treated the Jews? Are you really sure that the Almighty loves humankind more than he loves an ox?"

There was no purpose in this debate since the professor's wife was gone anyhow. I don't remember exactly how I spent the few hours in this town. If I'm not mistaken I took a sightseeing bus and went to some churches and historical sights. A few days passed and I found myself again in Rome. I went with a group of tourists to see a museum. Our guide stopped at a painting or a sculpture and began explaining its symbols and meanings. A few feet away another group entered with another guide and he, too, began to explicate some work of art. The men's voices intermingled. I looked up and saw the professor's wife. She stood in the other group and someone held her hand – a tall middle-aged man in sporty dress with a camera hanging from his shoulder. His crew cut hair was yellowish and so was his curly mustache. He had a snub nose and pale blue eyes. He kept whispering to her and kissing her earlobe. His clothes and his whole appearance were strictly European. Was he English, French, Swedish? One thing was clear to me, he was not her husband.

At first, I could not make out the language he was speaking. Then I heard that it was German. He certainly was not a German Jew. I said to the Evil One: "Here's the golden opportunity I missed. This man could have easily been a Nazi during the war. Men like this tore out the teeth of dying Jews for the bit of gold in their fillings. They took Jewish children from their cradles and dragged them to the ovens of Auschwitz."

But the Evil One has a dialectic mind and can always come up with the right answer. "This man might have been one of the few good Germans who saved Jews from the Nazi terror," he told me. "Besides, doesn't the Bible teach us to forgive and forget? How long should people remember the Holocaust?"

Translated by the author

NAVON

In Tel Aviv, I had found a distant relative from Poland, Isidore Baraband, who had first come to New York in 1946. In Warsaw, Isidore had been a lawyer. In New York, he was employed as a bookkeeper in a wine and liquor business for seventeen years. In 1963, he retired and went to Israel with his wife Zosia. Their son, Zygmunt, was in Madison, Wisconsin, where he taught Slavic languages at the university. Isidore Baraband was a big man, six feet tall, blond, good natured. At the age of sixty-seven, he did not have a single gray hair. He had lost, as he confided to me, all his ambitions and lived from his and Zosia's Social Security checks, and from a small annuity from an American insurance company. The lump sum of money paid to them by the German government was just enough to buy an apartment in an old building in Tel Aviv, not far from the sea, and Isidore got a dog, whom he called Navon.

Unlike Isidore, Zosia was small and thin. She had high cheek bones, a tiny nose and black eyes which seemed slanted and expressed the bitterness of a woman unable to make peace with her age and circumstances. Her hair dyed a dull black. Isidore spoke to me in Yiddish and even tried to throw in some sentences in Hebrew. He was in love, he told me, with the Jewish State, especially with Tel Aviv, which somehow reminded him of Warsaw. Zosia spoke only Polish, and she complained to me that Tel Aviv was dirty and that Hebrew was an Asiatic language that she could not learn in a hundred years.

In Hebrew, Navon is someone who is "understanding," and Isidore assured me that Navon possessed all the wisdom of a human and all the instincts of a beast. He was not kept at home, as dogs usually are in a big city. Instead, Isidore let him run free. Isidore had found him in Jaffa, an abandoned animal without a collar and tag, and he had brought him home with him. After a while, Isidore realized that Navon could take care of himself. He behaved more like a boarder or a grown son who puts in an appearance whenever he pleases. A full-blooded male, Navon was busy making love and waging war with other males. If he was given food in the house, he ate, and if not, he managed to find scraps of meat or bones in the garbage cans. He climbed up the three flights of stairs with the skill of a city dweller. If the door was not locked, he pressed the latch with his paw and entered. Mostly, he slept outside. I once watched Navon on Ben Yehuda Street waiting for the traffic light to change from red to green. He stood there with the patience of one who knows that it does not pay to risk one's life just to gain a few seconds.

I am not a specialist on dogs and their pedigrees, but Isidore told me that Navon belongs to a race which is native of Asia and is rarely found in Europe. According to Isidore, Navon had most probably come to Israel from Iraq, or perhaps from Iran. I remember him as a large dog, with a pointed muzzle, his fur a mixture of white and black, and with dark eyes that seemed to me incredibly smart. I often thought that he must be a reincarnation of some ancient sage.

All this took place in 1966. In 1969, I again visited Israel. I phoned Isidore from my hotel, and after I enquired about him and his wife, I asked, "How is Navon?"

Isidore began to stammer and choke, and then he was silent. After a while he said, "Navon committed suicide."

"Suicide? A dog? When? How?"

Isidore suddenly began to speak to me in a broken Hebrew, apparently so that Zosia would not understand. We made an appointment to meet me in a café on Dizengolf Street. The next day we met there. Isidore appeared thinner than the last time I'd seen him, his hair streaked with grey, and he had bags under his eyes. We ordered lemonade and Isidore said, "Since you last visit a bitter feud broke out in our house and Navon was its victim. The mere mentioning of his name makes me shudder, but we're relatives, and I shouldn't keep secrets from you.

"You must certainly have noticed that Zosia is not happy here. I am in love with this country, but she hates it. The food is no good. The people are loud, rude, and dishonest. The merchants are all cheats. The waiters in restaurants are utterly incompetent, the women are ugly, tastelessly dressed, a bunch of liars. You know well that in comparison with Warsaw or even New York, our winters are mild. But Zosia maintains that nowhere did she suffer from the cold more than here. In the summertime when a *hamsin* blows she becomes mortally sick or at least that's what she thinks. I don't need to tell you that it's all psychosomatic or self-hypnosis. One way or another she is unhappy, resentful, and always arguing.

"Not long after your last visit, we went through a crisis which almost put an end to our marriage. Zosia announced that she was going back to America once and for all, and if I intended to stay here, everything between us would be over. She had written alarming letters to our son. You know that the winters in Madison are like at the North Pole. I happened to visit there in January and the temperature had fallen to twenty below zero. I'd equipped myself with a woolen mask to wear over my face, a fur hat, a bulky knit sweater and galoshes, but I could not leave the house for days. In the summer the heat is even more oppressive than Tel Aviv. But according to Zosia, the climate there is ideal.

Zosia asked Zygmunt to rent her an apartment. I told Zosia, "If you want to go back, it's your choice. I'm staying here."

"For some time, Zosia behaved as if she wanted to leave. This seemed very strange to me. Like all couples, we had our differences, but generally speaking we avoided fights. You may consider me old-fashioned, but since I married her, I had, as they say, one God and one wife. At least physically, Zosia satisfied me. The fact that just now – in old age, when even people who have had a bad life together make up to escape lonesomeness – Zosia should become so independent, looked irrational to me. But there are no rules. Everyday Zosia repeated her ultimatum: 'Either come with me, or stay alone. If Tel Aviv is so dear to you, then our life together was a mistake to begin with,' and so on. I tried to reason with her that what happened to the Jews in Europe was proof that without a physical and spiritual home we were lost, but Zosia contended that these were empty phrases. I had never gone into any political debates with Zosia, but now we stayed awake nights discussing Zionism, Americanism, and everything else.

"Things don't happen quickly. In Madison, it's not easy to find an apartment, and especially not one Zosia wanted, both inexpensive and comfortable. They had racial conflicts and protests against the war in Vietnam. Zygmunt's letters were far from enthusiastic. His wife was probably too nervous to have her mother-in-law so close. You must be wondering what connection all this has with Navon. You will see soon.

"In February, 1967, my son already had a prospect of getting an apartment for his mother, and Zosia began to prepare for the trip. You must know that even though we are still American citizens, we hold the status of *Olim Hadashim*, new immigrants, and for us to leave the country is not as easy as for tourists. There is a special tax. As in all the newly founded states, we have quite a lot of red tape here. In the middle of all this, the Six-Day

War was about to break out. Now we know it was a six-day war. Actually, we lived in fear of war for many months. Nasser's generals threatened that we would all be driven into the sea. Zosia was half crazed with fear. I' gone through the First World War, the bombing of Warsaw, all kinds of danger and starvation in Russia. How much more could I take? And how could I help? I'll make it short. I decided to take a trip with Zosia and see for myself. Ten new difficulties arose. I had not renewed my passport and the American Embassy questioned my citizenship. Cables were rushed to Washington, and Washington was not in a hurry to reply. This is where Navon comes in.

"I forgot to tell you, or perhaps you noticed yourself, that Zosia's feelings towards Navon were not like mine. In the beginning, she loved him even more than I did, but then she cooled off. Why, I still don't know. Perhaps from sheer spite. Zosia claimed that Navon could bring sickness, that he stank, and other such false accusations. In reality, he was an exceptionally clean animal. He liked to be soaped and cleaned. I often went to the beach, and Navon used to accompany me. He was an excellent swimmer. I did not need to push him into the water. He splashed there all by himself. I used to throw a ball into the sea and Navon swam to get it. Zosia, who was afraid of the sea, might have simply been jealous of his skill, his independence, and who knows – of his male adventures. Navon almost never barked, he considered it beneath his dignity to bark like any other dog. But Zosia treated him so badly that he began to bark at her, and once he even snapped at her calf – at least she said so, although I saw no teeth marks. Don't ask me what a commotion she started. She became completely hysterical. She ran to a doctor and he sent her to a hospital to be tested for rabies. The neighbors had something to be upset about. Navon was excommunicated. Rumors were spread that he was crazy and ought to be shot.

"When we began to plan our trip to America, there was never any doubt in my mind that we would take Navon along. True, taking a dog on a plane involves expenses and difficulties. Some dogs are so scared that they get sick and even die. But leaving the animal behind was out of the question. Suddenly, Zosia told me that I could not take Navon with me, and that she would not let him into the house. There were new fights, and Zosia had such fits of fury that she got sick. She lay in bed and wailed that because of Navon, she would die. She uttered such absurdities and went into such rages that I considered taking her to a psychiatrist. You wouldn't believe me, nor would anybody else, but Navon knew what was happening. He became sad and his eyes seemed to ask, "What have I done to deserve such hatred?" He stopped coming to the stairs each night. Animals know and understand more than we believe.

"We had a neighbor in the house, Zeinvel Amsterdam, an unlikeable fellow, a former smuggler. In the war he lost his wife and children and stayed in a German Displaced Persons Camp. His wife Regina was a real shrew, sly and noisy. She spoke only Polish. There's an entire group of Polish Yentas here who sit in the cafés on Dizengoff all day long and chatter away in Polish, imagining that they are still in Poland, where they were despised. They've kept their exile mentality. Thank God, their children are normal human beings. Some of them reached high positions in the army and air force. That same Regina has a son from her first marriage who is a professor at the Hebrew University of Jerusalem.

"When Regina learned that we were about to leave for America and we didn't know what to do with the dog, she proposed to take Navon. In the last few years there were many burglaries. Regina expected Navon to guard her apartment. Zosia was more than willing to accept this proposal. They'd made the decision without my knowing. Already, Regina began to babble to Navon in Polish, to treat him to greasy leftovers, and tried to lead him on a leash. But Navon showed little enthusiasm for her advantages and even for her tidbits. He actually bit her, and this time one could see his teeth marks on her flesh. When I heard what was happening, I said that I would rather see Navon dead than have him fall into Regina's hands. She would have kept him imprisoned. I happen to know what prison can do to you. The Bolsheviks put me in jail for eight months without an indictment and I did not intend to let Navon become a prisoner. There were new scenes, and the Amsterdams stopped talking to me. In the middle of all this, the Six-Day War broke out.

"During the few days that the war lasted, Zosia accused me of trapping her in Tel Aviv because of the dog. It was a lie. The professor in Madison who was to have sublet his house had postponed his trip because he was invited to teach in Japan. If I'm not mistaken, his child became sick. I don't remember the exact details.

"At the end of June, both of us were ready, but this time Navon really was the cause of the delay. Zosia was adamant that Navon should not go with us. We argued every night, and Zosia was again on the verge of going without me. Navon had disappeared for days, and I began to worry that he had been stolen, or run over by a car. One morning, when I was about to go to the beach, I opened the door and saw Navon.

He was standing at the threshold, waiting for me. I will never forget the expression in his eyes. There was guilt in them, and shyness. As a rule Navon, was not inclined to show me too much love. He wasn't the kind of dog who jumps all over his owner and licks him. His greatest show of tenderness was lifting up a paw and putting it in my hand. Now he stood up on his hind legs and put both paws on me.

Zosia had fallen asleep at dawn and I brought Navon into the kitchen and gave him some dog food and a bowel of water. He seemed thin and I thought that he must be starved, but he looked at the food and then at me as if apologizing for not eating. He only drank a little water.

I told him that I was going to the beach and he followed me. It was a warm day. I went into the water and Navon went after me. He began to swim, and from time to time, he turned his head as if to say, "Look at what I'm doing!" I did not suspect anything. I got out of the water and watched a military aircraft heading toward the airport, like those that made mincemeat of Nasser's forces. I looked again and saw that Navon had swum out farther than ever. I could barely see his head. He was moving away from the shore with uncanny determination. I ran after him and called him to come back, but he no longer looked back. At that moment I knew the bitter truth – Navon was committing suicide. He soon vanished and was never found. Navon understood that he was in our way, and did away with himself. There is not and cannot be any other explanation."

Isidore turned silent. He drank what was left of his lemonade. I looked up to a balcony across the street in order not to see his eyes. He bent his head and muttered something into the table, and into the two empty glasses. After a while, he said, "The sacrifice was not necessary. A day before we were about to leave, a cable came from Zygmunt saying that he had been awarded a Fulbright and that he was going with his wife to English. There was no point going to Madison while our son was going to be abroad for at least a year. The whole plan came to nothing. You won't believe it, but Zosia made a lot of noise, accusing me of drowning the dog in order not to leave him with Regina. These are the bare facts.

"We somehow made peace. At our age it's too late to make changes. And besides, not everyone has the wisdom and courage of a Navon."

Translated by the author and Alma Singer

A LETTER TO MAMA

The older he became, the less able Sam Metzger was to understand why he had never written to his mother after leaving Krasnobrod for America. This "letter to mama," which he never wrote, became the bane of his existence. Granted that he disliked writing letters and that the first years in New York he used to work fifteen hours a day in a sweat shop. Still, to leave his widowed mother behind in Krasnobrod, and never write her so much as a single word, he had to be out of his mind. Sam could not fathom how this came about although he had brooded over it many sleepless nights.

At first it was simply a manner of putting it off. Then he seemed to forget about it altogether. At night, while trying to fall asleep in Moishe Leckechbecker's alcove on Attorney Street, along with three other boarders, he would think of it. In the morning he would forget again. Later the nagging sense of shame turned into conviction that it was already too late. A devil possessed him who wouldn't let him take a pen in hand. In New York at the time, they were all singing a popular Yiddish song which went: "Why delay? Write your mother today." From the Yiddish theater stage, from Second Avenue cabarets, in the workshops on Grand Street, from record players blaring in homes, the song followed him everywhere.

Perhaps that was the reason Sam left New York. He got as far as Chicago, where he became a peddler. He knew no fellow countrymen from Krasnobrod there. He married a Lithuanian girl, a plump orphan named Bessie, and his business prospered. Bessie had saved nine hundred dollars with which she opened a women's wear shop. Sam and a partner bought a store which handled the same sort of merchandise.

Miracles didn't happen to Sam. He didn't become a Rockefeller. He and his wife needed little and managed to earn three or four times more than they needed. When they were in their thirties, a daughter was born to them whom Bessie named Sylvia – after her own mother, Sarah. The couple hired a Polish servant, Antosia, who became devoted to the child. Antosia's husband, a coal miner, had died in a pit. They had had no children. Antosia was more trustworthy than a relative of the family could ever be. She ran the household, cared for Sylvia, and was frugal. She invested her savings in Sam's business, eventually accumulating several thousand dollars. Whenever Sam would try to pay her salary, she would argue, "What good is money to me? I have everything." She drew up a will in which Sylvia became her sole beneficiary.

Later, Sam bought a department store in a city in Illinois where no more than twenty Jewish families lived, mostly business people, a few professionals, a doctor, a dentist, and a veterinarian. During the day the men were occupied with their work. At night they played cards. After a while, they hired a rabbi and established a synagogue, but there were never enough men attending to make up a minyan, except for Rosh Hashanah and Yom Kippur. The rabbi, a bachelor, was openly living with a gentile girl. Everyone called him by his first name, Jack. In the late twenties, fundraisers began coming from Chicago, New York, even from Palestine, all demanding large donations. They reprimanded the Jews for not giving their children a proper upbringing. But there were hardly any Jewish children left, only grandchildren of mixed marriages.

Sylvia had grown up and had gone off to college. Sam was approaching sixty. The years had been filled with business, card playing, and an occasional trip to California or Florida. Antosia had died and Sylvia had inherited her money. Sam set an elaborate tombstone over Antosia's grave in the Catholic cemetery.

Over the years, Sam had managed to avoid contact with anyone from Krasnobrod. He had no idea whether his mother had died and whether he should say Kaddish and light an anniversary candle for her. He kept from mentioning the word Krasnobrod among the town Jews, even though they probably wouldn't have know where it was since they all were born either in Lithuania or Rumania.

In his effort to forget, Sam had become a traitor to his people. Several of the Jewish spokesmen who visited the town from time to time would refer to the community as godless, materialistic, money-grubbing. The other men resented these rebukes, but Sam Metzger reluctantly agreed.

During the day Sam was too busy to think about these things, but at night, after the card playing, lying beside Bessie in the upstairs bedroom, his thoughts would assail him like a swarm of locust.

Sam owned a $60,000 home with a large garden and a two-car garage for his and Bessie's Cadillacs. Sylvia was at school in California. Bessie now needed a pill before going to bed. Sam was in the habit of taking a warm bath at bedtime. This late-night bath had become for him an hour of reflection.

Every time he undressed and saw himself naked in the mirror on the dresser or on the door, he would make a short reckoning of his life. He had been lucky, but had aged prematurely. His round, bald head was ringed with sparse white hair. His crooked nose was covered with drunkard's warts although he seldom drank. Loose flaps of skin hung beneath his brown eyes and he had a flabby double chin. His legs were bowed and too short. His toenails were twisted and yellowish.

Occasionally after his bath, he would sit down in the dinette and drink a glass of orange juice. A photograph of Sylvia hung there. The girl was the image of her grandmother, the very one to whom Sam did not write.

It was impossible to escape his mother. She sprang up before him over and over again in his new house. The resemblance was apparent the moment the nurse brought the newborn Sylvia to him in the Chicago hospital. Sam felt a love for this child which he knew was excessive.

Once Sylvia started to walk she showed how capricious and contrary she would be. Sam was almost convinced that the girl was repaying him for the wrong done her grandmother.

Now Sylvia was planning to marry a gentile, a sportsman who won medals at racing sailboats, the son of a rich engineer. She had confessed to her mother that she was living with him and had already had an abortion. Sam's love for Sylvia was spoiled. The fortune he had amassed through the toil of a lifetime would eventually pass into the hands of this stranger who looked down at Sam from his six-foot-two inch height with contempt.

But who else could he make his heir? The fundraisers who came to town using threats to raise money? The American Jewish organizations, whose red-nailed secretaries clicked away at typewriters, and where directors received enormous salaries? His visits to Chicago, his reading of newspapers, and his own observations had convinced Sam Metzger that money given to charity was mainly spent to keep the organizations going. Even in his own city contributions were used to further personal ambitions. The president of the synagogue had hired his son-in-law as the architect for the new building. Another influential member had brought in a brother-in-law with a hoarse voice to be the Cantor. The rabbi was also someone's relative. They had overpaid for the site of the Jewish Center and for building materials. The son-in-law architect had designed a synagogue which resembled a bat.

This night, as on all the other nights, Sam Metzger sipped his orange juice and smoked a last cigar, though the doctor had forbidden him to smoke. Instead of losing weight, he was getting heavier. He and Bessie often quarreled about the bedroom temperature. He was always too hot and she too cold. He had high blood pressure. An artery in his left eye had burst and he had to be on medications and stick to a diet.

He was beginning to lose his hearing and had to wear a hearing aid. He had to carry two pairs of eyeglasses with him: bifocals as well as sunglasses. He constantly was switching from one to the other or misplacing them. He could find no shoes that fit him properly. Sooner or later every pair began to pinch his feet. Somehow he was always taking medicine – for gas, constipation, headaches, stomach cramps.

In her middle age, Bessie had lost interest in Sam altogether. She lived only for her daughter, catering to her every whim. They had more than their share of problems in the business. Thefts, inefficiency, wasteful competition, and quarrels. If Sam stayed away from the business so much as a day, everything went wrong. Despite her intelligence, Bessie was a woman with devious ways and stubborn as a mule.

"Well," he thought, "the whole thing is going to fall to pieces. Nothing will be left to show for all my hard work."

He vaguely recalled several biblical passages from the time he attended Hebrew school in Krasnobrod, but he couldn't remember the exact words. It all amounted to the idea that life was barren and nonsensical. A person took nothing with him to the grave but the sins he had committed against man and God.

Sam continued to sit quietly. Should he take a sleeping pill? Or should he try to get along without one tonight? He decided to take one. Nothing frightened him as much as lying awake at night, thinking. During the day, Krasnobrod and even New York were far off, but at night the years seemed to shrink. He remembered all his troubles and those of others. Sooner or later the tune, "A Letter to Mama," would start running through his head.

Sam snuffed out his cigar in the remainder of the orange juice, shut off the light, and with heavy steps walked up to his bedroom. Bessie was snoring. He got into his bed and immediately felt too hot. Bessie had promised him she would turn off the radiator, but it was apparently still on. He kicked off the blanket and lay uncovered as if it were summer.

He was tired but his thoughts kept him awake. For years he had talked of retiring from the business. Were he to live to a hundred, he would have enough money. But what would he do with himself after he sold everything? Where would he live? He had already tried Miami and Santa Barbara. The idleness soon became boring. It was difficult to find a good partner at cards. He had heard a great deal about the Riviera, but how could he learn to speak French at his age?

Sam pictured his daughter, Sylvia, in bed with her Gentile, caressing him, giving herself to him. Perhaps he was talking against him, her father, and she was covering his mouth with kisses. "Well, it's all over, all over," Sam muttered to himself, not knowing himself what he meant by these words. Drowsy he lay quietly, looking straight ahead, and saw at the foot of the bed a familiar form, a woman. He found himself staring at her, his mind empty of thoughts, not registering any surprise. A glow emanated from her in the dark. She stood as in a half-lit portrait. Suddenly she approached him, not walking, but drifting between him and the heavily-draped windows. He noted that instead of eyes there were two green phosphorescent lights in her sockets. When she spoke it was as if he heard her with his entire being and not with his ears alone.

"Shmulik, it's me..."

At the sound of his mother's voice Sam's body shuddered. He wanted to cry out, "Mama!" but could utter no sound. At once the vision began to fade. It retreated, became dim, indistinct and in a moment gone altogether. The darkness returned and he again became aware of Bessie's snoring. He lay motionless staring in amazement at the spot where the visitor had just stood. "It's Mama, Mama!" he muttered to himself, "She's come to get me... She's forgiven me..."

He remained awake for a considerable time, waiting. Perhaps she would reappear. But she did not show herself again. He tried to recall details. How was she dressed? Was she wearing a wig or a head-covering? Did she have on a skirt, a shawl? He could remember nothing. Could it have been a dream? But he knew he had been awake. He pondered the event until he was overcome with fatigue and fell asleep.

The alarm clock rang and out of one eye Sam could see Bessie getting up. Every morning she opened the store herself, not letting anyone forget that she was the owner. Now she sat on the edge of the bed, her uncombed hair a mixture of brown, red, and gray. Unkempt and haggard, she looked her very worst those first few minutes after the alarm clock rang. Her eye makeup had dried overnight and was like cracked plaster on a wall. Her forehead was wrinkled. Her lower chin sagged. Her nose seemed even more pointed than usual. Her mouth, without her teeth, was sunken and shut tight. In the semi-darkness, Bessie's black eyes, surrounded with wrinkles and dark shadows, reminded Sam of two black coals *heder* boys in Krasnobrod used to set in a snowman's head.

For a few seconds, Bessie hesitated, as if debating whether it was worth getting up or not. Then she stood up. Her body was fat and flabby while her legs were thin and varicosed. She walked unsteadily to the bathroom. Sam's gaze followed her but he soon shut his eyes. There was only one bathroom upstairs, and though Bessie didn't mind his sharing it with her, he preferred to wait till she had washed, bathed, and was out of the house before using it himself. She never ate breakfast, just drank a glass of milk.

For a moment, Sam didn't remember what had happened to him during the night. Like every other morning, he awoke feeling insufficiently rested, with a bitter taste in his mouth which came from his bile, his liver, or perhaps from his soul. He lived in hope that the day would come when the ringing of the alarm clock wouldn't startle him each morning, but that day was yet to come.

Now he could neither fall back asleep nor really wake up. He furrowed his brow in an effort to force himself to sleep. "What time is it, eh?" he wondered, too lazy and too indifferent to look at the clock. Surprisingly, he did doze off but soon awoke with a start. Bessie must have left the house because he heard nothing from the bathroom or kitchen.

Suddenly, remembering the apparition, Sam sat bolt upright. God in Heaven! This was no ordinary morning! This was like Yom Kippur morning, where even here, in this godforsaken town, every Jew went to pray in the synagogue. There was something unusual in the air – something unidentifiably cool and heavy.

Ordinarily, Sam would fix himself a breakfast of orange juice, a roll, and coffee after Bessie's departure, but today he had no appetite. He shaved and bathed. Standing in front of the mirror, scratching his beard, which seemed to become rougher from day to day, he came to a decision: he would go to New York, look up the Krasnobrod people, and find out the truth about his mother once and for all.

"My God, I still have relatives somewhere who most probably need me, need help," Sam said to himself. "Maybe that's why Mama came to me, to get me to help them. For a few thousand dollars, I might save lives!"

His conscience, which had been asleep for so many years, had awakened. "I'll leave them enough! More than enough!" Sam spoke aloud. He was referring to Bessie and Sylvia. "She can even remarry," ran through his mind. The painful possibility that Bessie might marry his enemy, his chief competitor, Bill Weintraub, a recent widower, occurred to him. Such things happened every day.

Sam tried to conjure up how Bessie and Weintraub would look together in the local newspaper photo above an article describing the merger of their businesses. "Maybe it's not too late!" Same called out, not really knowing what he was referring to. "Changing the will isn't enough. Once I'm dead, a mere bribe can make a judge annul everything. A person has to do good deeds as long as he can stand on his feet. God Almighty has made it possible for me to fulfill this task."

Sam Metzger dressed, packed some underwear, a sweater and the medicines he would need. A long-forgotten energy awoke in him. The strength of a man who knows that he must act vigorously or lose everything. Bessie had left breakfast for him on the kitchen table but he had no desire either for food or coffee. Though it was a winter day, the frost had somewhat melted. In mid-February, it smelled of Spring. Sam had shaved and bathed in minutes. He went to the bank and had a part of his account transferred to a New York bank, a procedure which necessitated the signing of many papers. He told the bank official he had a chance to buy a business in New York. Sam knew full well that the news would soon spread all over town, but what did he care about small-town gossip? Let Bill Weintraub have something to think about.

Sam went into a telephone booth and called Bessie, saying, "Bessie! I'm going to New York!"

The two of them still conversed in Yiddish. Bessie was silent for a while. "What's happened?"

"My mother died."

"Only now? How do you know?"

"I received word."

"So what will you do in New York? After all, she's in Poland, not in New York."

Bessie argued that he couldn't leave at this time. They were getting ready for a big sale. She couldn't be everywhere. She shouted at him in her Lithuanian dialect, calling him names. But Sam yelled back and hung up, almost saying, "Let Bill Weintraub help you!"

Aside from the special excitement he was experiencing, he felt a long-forgotten wanderlust, a boyish thrill at the thought of being free. He had bought $5,000 worth of traveler's checks. A train was leaving for Chicago in a half an hour. He walked out of the bank and took a cab to the railroad station, arriving in enough time to have a sandwich and a cup of coffee. "What in heaven's name led me to waste my life in this good-for-nothing hole? What was I hiding from? Where was my brain?"

The train was warm and spacious. Sam looked out of the window at the snow-covered fields. In contrast to his lifelong habit of frugality and saving, Sam was now eager to spend money. He would go to the Krasnobrod Society in New York and donate a large sum towards relief. He would fly by plane to Poland. What could possibly happen to him? He was old and sick. He wasn't even afraid of Hitler, who threatened Poland with war. He would travel to Krasnobrod and find his relatives there. Then he would bring them to the American consulate in Warsaw and see to it that they all obtained visas. He would rescue as many as possible.

The words of the spokesmen of the Zionist organizations, even though he had never really listened to them, now came back to mind with new force, as if he were hearing them for the first time. They repeated themselves like a record being played over and over again: "Our suffering brothers are waiting. They are our flesh and blood. If American Jewry doesn't help, what then ... "

"How could I have heard those pleas and remained indifferent?" Sam asked himself. True, to those delegates it was just a business. They got a percentage. But what they were saying was nevertheless true. Who would help if not he? Who should be concerned about Krasnobrod – Hitler?

Sam could hardly wait for the train to arrive in Chicago. At the station he inquired about a flight to New York. Somehow, everything fell into place. He took a cab and drove to the airport. Ten minutes later he was airborne. "Will the plane crash? Let it," Sam thought. He felt no fear at all, remembering a saying that those who go on a mission of mercy are protected.

The plane flew into a snowstorm and started to roll from side to side, but Sam continued to sip the cocktail the stewardess had served him. Seeing that other passengers were anxious, he smiled to himself. Next to him sat a young woman wearing a sable coat and a Russian style fur hat, a *papakha*.

Sam said to her, "We'll soon be landing in New York."

"Either in New York or in a snowy grave," she answered.

"Everything happens according to God's will," Sam said, a little surprised at his own words.

"The question is: what is God's will?" she replied dryly.

A clever woman, Sam thought. What does God want? Who would dare go to heaven and ask God to tell him His desire?

Patches of fog drifted past the window. The pilot tried to lift the plane above the storm clouds but apparently wasn't able to manage it. In a matter of seconds it became dark as night outside. Sam imagined the motors were operating on their last bit of fuel. The wind was blowing against them from the Atlantic Ocean. The hostess had disappeared as if she felt personally responsible for having trapped the passengers in this dangerous situation.

The woman in the sable said to Sam, "Better fasten your safety belt."

"What good will it do me?" Sam gestured with his hand, expressing paternal gratitude. She is more devoted than Sylvia, he thought. Sylvia, in her place, wouldn't have given him so much as a glance.

The plane bumped down on the runway and came to a stop in the New York airport. Sam said to the woman, "Now you know what God desires."

"Yes, now I know."

Some men have all the luck, Sam mused. I've thrown away my best years struggling with that dried up Lithuanian wife of mine, stuck in a town where everyone knows what's cooking in everyone else's pot.

His eyes followed the handsome woman, admiring her shapely legs. A tall man wearing a Homburg greeted her. They must be aristocrats, society people, Sam decided. Perhaps he's a diplomat.

It was already evening and the airport was brightly lit. Outdoors it was cold and foggy. The planes waiting to take off to all parts of the world looked fantastically huge. It still was impossible for Sam to comprehend how such immense and heavy structures could fly across oceans and deserts. Overnight a machine like the one he was on could take him to Krasnobrod.

It occurred to Sam that he didn't have a passport. He hadn't even taken his citizenship papers with him. Carrying his suitcase, he walked through an enormous waiting room. Unlike a railway station, where the waiting passengers are warmly clad, laden with packages, the people here were wearing light-weight clothing, as if they were all flying to some mild climate. They carried small suitcases or attaché cases. It was airy and warm. Young men and women stood about in small groups, chatting casually. People here didn't seem terribly concerned with the frightening conditions in every part of the world.

Sam went outside and took a taxi. He could tell that the cab driver was Jewish. He asked him, "Are you Jewish?"

"Sure. What else?"

"Take me where I can find some Jews."

"New York is full of Jews."

"Where do people from the old country get together? Do you by any chance know where any Jews from Krasnobrod meet?"

"Are you crazy, or are you putting on an act? Tell me where you want to go."

"Where is the Yiddish newspaper office?"

"Mister, I'll take you down to Second Avenue, to the Café Royal. You'll find lots of newspaper men there."

The driver pushed down the flag on the meter. Sam leaned his head against the side of the cab, affected by the overwhelming odor of tobacco. He rolled the window down a bit. It had been years since he was last in New York and he hardly recognized the city. He had never really known it. The streets seemed narrower and the buildings taller. There was a hint of the nearby ocean in the air, which smelled of gasoline, exhaust fumes, and all the pungent odors of city life.

Early in the day it had been warmer but it was turning colder now. The radio predicted a snowstorm. Sam knew that he should first have made hotel reservations, but he decided that there were plenty of hotels in New York. Now that he was here, he was anxious to be among Jews as quickly as possible. There had been a time when he had lived, worked, attended meetings in this city. He had taken up with a girl who had been a passenger on the same boat from Europe with him. He had kissed her, even planned to marry her, but through the years he had forgotten all the names and all the addresses. The girl was his age, perhaps a bit older. She was undoubtedly a grandmother by this time.

Sam shut his eyes, letting the cool wind blow across his forehead and eyelids. He inhaled the city air. He couldn't believe he was actually making this trip.

After a long silence, the drive spoke, "You're homesick for Jews, eh?"

Sam started. "It's been thirty years since I've been here."

"Tomorrow you can go to the Yiddish newspaper office. They'll fill you in on everything."

"You've never heard of Krasnobrod?"

"Krasnobrod? No, my dad came from a town near Minsk."

"And your mother?"

"My mother? I don't know. From somewhere in Russia . . . "

The driver grumbled continuously, scolding other drivers. He blew his horn loudly at a truck which was holding up traffic and zigzagged around it, almost knocking down a pedestrian. He never stopped cursing: "Sons of bitches . . . They should break their legs."

When the taxi drove down Second Avenue, Sam thought he recognized the street. He saw restaurants with baskets of rolls on the tables, store windows displaying knishes, bagels, egg-kichel, challah, apple strudel. He could almost smell the gefilte fish, peppered chick-peas, sauerkraut, all familiar Krasnobrod dishes. Young boys were hawking Yiddish newspapers. On a theater marquee there was brightly lit Yiddish lettering.

Sam Metzger's eyes filled with tears.

Jews go on living here while he wasted his years in exile. He could hardly wait for the taxi to come to a halt. The meter indicated $2.80 but Sam handed the driver a five-dollar bill and told him to keep the change. The man was so astonished that he forgot to thank him.

Sam spotted the Café Royal. Around here is where I'll stay, Sam decided. I'll get an apartment. Let Bessie sue me for divorce. He stood on the street, staring up at the reddening sky, at the theater billboards, at the crowd which was milling around the box office. He walked into the café and heard Yiddish spoken. People were sitting at tables, shouting and apparently arguing. Sam looked for an empty table, but they were all occupied. Having come into this heated place from the cold his eyes teared up and everything appeared blurred. The room began to spin like a carousel. Gradually things came into focus. Women sat at the tables dressed like actresses, their faces thick with make-up and their eyes blue with eye-shadow, but they spoke the mother tongue. One of them, a heavy-set woman, took out a jeweled lipstick case from her purse and carefully applied lipstick to her already red lips. On one finger, with a bright red nail, a stone sparkled with the colors of the rainbow. When the waiter approached her for her order, she commanded him with one word:

"Blintzes!"

Sam was on the verge of tears. Blintzes? He felt shaky, as if he were drunk. He walked up to a table at which several men were sitting and said, "Is Yiddish still spoken here? I want to hear it."

"Where do you come from?" a big man with a red face, bulging eyes and childlike blond curls asked him.

Sam told him.

"Maybe you'd like to buy a Yiddish book?"

"Sure."

"Have a chair, sit down. Hey, boys, let the man sit down! That's the way. If you're hungry, you can order what your heart desires. What would you like? Here, you can get matzo-brei any time of the year."

"I hear you can get blintzes here."

"As much as you can put away."

"Can I … may I … order for everyone?"

"Move in a little closer. Fellows, who wants blintzes? Here, this is my book. It just came out in print. Poetry."

"Poetry?"

Sam had more than once heard the word poetry but what it was he had forgotten. The man removed a yellow book with gold engraved letters from his briefcase and said, "Would you like me to autograph it? It costs $25.00."

"Sure."

Sam took a wallet full of bank notes from his jacket. His hands trembled. He had no $5 bills, only ten, twenty and fifty dollar bills. He handed the man $30 wanting to say something in Yiddish but all he could muster was "That's for good luck ... "

He felt an acute pang of embarrassment. Sam had never learned how to speak English properly. How often he had made a fool of himself in front of Sylvia's friends with his bad English. And now he had half forgotten his Yiddish.

The big man with the gold stitched tie, the author, took out a fountain pen and wrote a long inscription in the inside cover, sticking the tip of his tongue out of the corner of his mouth as he did so. The waiter arrived with the blintzes.

More authors with their books joined the table and Sam bought a book from each of them. He accumulated a whole pile. The writers soon resumed their interrupted debate. Though Sam understood the words, he couldn't comprehend what these intellectuals were debating. They were accusing someone of plagiarizing entire passages from Yesenin. Who is this Yesenin, Sam wanted to ask. He opened one of the books and tried to read it, but though it was printed in Yiddish, he was unable to understand it. The words didn't seem to go together. The lines of print danced in front of his eyes, seeming to change colors. Am I going blind? Sam thought. His throat felt dry. There was a tight feeling in his chest. He had forgotten to take his pills with him. He asked, "Do you have any idea where I can find dome people from Krasnobrod?"

"Where is this Krasnobrod?"

"I'm from Krasnobrod." Someone spoke up. It was the voice of a woman at a nearby table, the same one who had been applying the lipstick. Sam sat up.

"Are you from Krasnobrod?"

"Who are you?"

"Say, everybody, let's push the tables together!" The big man with the blond curls called out, "It's about time the writers and the actors' tribe got a little closer."

There was much gay conversation and laughter as the tables were pushed together. Sam asked, "How many years since you were in Krasnobrod?"

"Never ask a woman about years. What's your name?"

"Sam – I mean – Shmuel Metzger. My mother, may she rest in peace, was called Belle Itte, Bracha's daughter."

"Was our father a butcher?"

"A butcher? No, my father died when I was a boy."

"How did your mother manage?"

"She would go to the village to buy some buckwheat or a goose."

"When did you come to America?"

Sam told her when.

"That's before my time. Where did you live in Krasnobrod?"

"On the street near the hill." Sam replied.

"Near the meat market?"

"No. The pines. What was your father's name?" Sam asked, barely able to speak, as if afraid of what her answer might be.

"Malech Berl Altele's son. We sold oats and flax. Where did you live?"

"Near the bridge."

"What bridge?"

The longer the two of them spoke the more confused both of them became. Sam mopped the perspiration from his brow.

The actress rummaged through her purse and took her lipstick out again.

"Where in the world is your Krasnobrod?" she asked impatiently.

"In the Lublin region."

"I'm from the Czernichow area."

"Mazel-tov, there are two Krasnobrods!" The big man shouted, clapping his hands together.

"Hey, waiter!"

Sam stood up. He asked where the bathroom was. He had to urinate and he had to cry.

It was late when Sam Metzger left the Café Royal with his load of books. I didn't know books could be so heavy, he though in amazement. The appetizing smells of fresh bagel and coffee came from a nearby restaurant. Newsboys were shouting the next morning headlines of the Yiddish newspapers. As he mingled with the crowd emerging from a Yiddish theater, he heard people in avid Yiddish arguing over the merits of the play. Couples strolled arm in arm, some pausing to buy a newspaper. They know how to live, Sam thought. I buried myself in some wilderness. It had been years since he and Bessie had walked arm in arm. As soon as he so much as touched her, she would protest, as if he had stepped on her foot or messed up her hairdo. She could only ridicule him and incite her daughter against him.

Sam bought a newspaper. On the front page was a headline about Palestine. Why don't I visit Palestine, he asked himself. Sam paused in front of the window of a Yiddish bookstore which also sold sheet music. He would have loved to go in, but it was closed. A fine, needle-sharp snow started to fall. In a moment, the crowded street emptied except for a few drunkards who looked to him like actors on a stage set. A strong wind blew. A page of a Yiddish newspaper lifted into the air, tried to fly up to the dark red sky, fell back to earth again, spun around and came to rest at Sam's foot. Maybe it's a message, he thought, a letter from Heaven. He wanted to stoop over and pick it up but his back wouldn't bend. What kinds of thoughts are filling my head, he wondered.

A taxi drove up and Sam stepped in. Sam read the driver's name, David Cohen, on his back license. Sam said, "Take me to a Jewish hotel, Mr. Cohen."

"Do you want Kosher food?"

"What? Yes, Kosher."

"Well, on Broadway and Fourth Street there's a Kosher hotel. Rabbis hold conventions there."

"Okay. Take me there."

"I once took three Rabbis there. Polish refugees."

"Have you ever heard of anyone from Krasnobrod?"

"Oh, you'll find out about everything at this place."

A few minutes later the cab stopped in front of a hotel. Sam went up to the registration desk and asked for a room. The clerk handed him a form to fill out and a bell-hop took him up on the elevator. As they passed one floor, Sam could hear loud voices and music, and the foot-stomping of a party.

He went into his room, set down his books, tipped the bell-hop a dollar, and was given a key. This transaction took no more than a few minutes. He put his reading glasses on, opened one of the books, read a few of the phrases, and shut it again. They eat blintzes like everyone else, he thought, but their ideas are very difficult.

He had to use the bathroom again. Where does all this liquid come from? I don't remember having drunk so much. He knew the truth: he had an enlarged prostate. The doctor had recommended surgery, predicting complications if it were ignored. Sam's heart was getting weaker, not stronger.

He wanted to undress but he was too tired, so he just took off his coat and shoes, stretched out on the bed and shut the light. It was warm in the room, the steam hissed in the radiator on one monotonous plaintive note. Sam imagined that the steam was complaining,

I'm uncomfortable, I'm miserable, I can't get out, I can't get out. No one can help me, not even God. I must suffer, suffer…

The dance music from below became louder. Sam thought he heard a familiar melody which he recalled being played at Krasnobrod weddings. He wasn't sure exactly what it was: the wedding march to the chuppah? A scissor dance? An anger dance? Sam listened intensely. This music seemed to be played by home-town musicians, magically transporting him to Krasnobrod. He saw the faces of relatives, neighbors, teachers, classmates. He pictured the rabbi with his white beard, his puffy cheeks with fine blue veins, his thick white eyebrows and heavily lined forehead. The old man smiled blissfully, a grandfatherly indulgence radiating from his eyes.

The melodies followed one after the other, and Sam knew them all. Perhaps he just imagined he did. He had heard them back home. He found himself singing along, humming the tunes. The party grew noisy. He could hear laughter, bursts of applause, loud masculine pronouncements, responsive feminine giggling. This was not a party, but a wedding. In New York, people led a Jewish life, married their children according to Jewish traditions, had Jewish in-laws.

The band stopped and then struck up again. God in Heaven, they were playing "A Letter to Mama." As soon as Sam heard this tune, his face was bathed with tears. A miracle had happened, a miracle! He had come to New York and on his very first night they had played a song that had constantly echoed in his ears. Sylvia, who had played the piano and had studied some music, had referred to this song as "junk." But how can "junk" uplift the soul, fill it with a longing and love beyond description? Sam had the urge to go down to the wedding, to congratulate the bride and groom, to mingle with the guests. He was tired, but not sleepy. He got off the bed. His legs felt unsteady but just the same he switched on the light, found his shoes and went out into the hall. He rang for the elevator and waited a long time, but it didn't come.

Sam walked down the stairs, figuring that on the floor below he would find the wedding, but the corridor was dark and quiet. He walked down another flight but there was no wedding there either. For a moment he stood unbelievingly. Is the wedding over? he asked himself. He decided to walk down one more floor but with the same result.

He rang for the elevator again, waited and still it didn't come. What kind of service is this? Sam muttered. Well, I might as well go down to the lobby.

He went down a few more floors without reaching the lobby. Instead he found himself in the basement. There were lights on but the place was empty. Folding chairs were stacked along the walls. Sand-filled ashtrays held cigarette stubs. Smoke was still trailing from one of the cigarette, a sign that someone had just been there. No elevator door could be seen.

He wanted to go up to the lobby, but he needed to rest for a moment. For the past few years, he'd lived in constant fear of a heart attack. Climbing up and down stairs was too taxing for him. He was beginning to regret having gone in search of this strange wedding. Well, they must have finished their dancing. As he sat there, his mind vacant, he felt a vibration and hollowness in his knees, as if he had just climbed up, not down, all these stairs. He was suddenly overcome by all that had happened to him during the past twenty-four hours. If yesterday at this time, someone would have told him that the next day he would be in a New York hotel, searching for a wedding, sitting alone in a basement, he would have considered him mad.

He looked up and saw a pay phone. An urge to call Bessie took hold of him. She was, after all, his wife. She might be worried about him. He inserted a dime, intending to call collect, but didn't hear the usual dial tone. The phone was apparently out of order. He clicked the receiver cradle up and down to get his coin back but nothing happened. When men make something, you can be sure it will know how to steal, Sam mused.

At that moment everything became dark. It seemed someone upstairs had shut the lights. Sam shouted "Hey, you! Put the lights on! Hey, mister! Let me out!" He started to walk but couldn't make out the exit. Like a blind man, he felt his way in the dark. He began to panic. His heart beat loudly. He could no longer remain standing. He had to sit down. His body broke into a cold sweat and severe nausea gripped him.

He felt the ground and heard the dull thud of his body against the floor. Then it became still – a stillness outside of himself as well as inside. He lay quietly, not knowing whether he had fainted or just fallen. Is this a heart attack, he asked himself. If so, it isn't so terrible. It's probably gas, from the blintzes.

A sense of peace descended upon him. He shut his eyes. He listened to his innermost self. His desires, his regrets, left him. He knew now that Bessie would marry Bill Weintraub, yet he felt no anger towards them. What's the poor woman to do?

His mother reappeared, but something had changed. She and Sylvia were one and the same woman. How come I didn't understand this before? he asked himself.

He became light and started to fly into the night. He flew past the New York skyscrapers. Together with his mother he flew over a congealed ocean. Down below, ships stood motionless. Then mother and son approached a path between two mountains. In the valley, he saw something shining like a brilliant red sunrise. Where is my father? he asked himself and heard the answer, You, Sam, are your own father.

At the border, an unseen power held him back, but his mother embraced him. Together, arm in arm, they floated back to Krasnobrod.

Translated by Aliza Shevrin

Original English publication in chronological order, followed by title and date of Yiddish publication, which, unless otherwise noted, appeared in the Forverts*:*

"The Lost Wife," *The Critic*, Octtober-November 1968 ("Dos farloyrene vayb": Dec 3, 4, 1965)

"Advice," *Israel Magazine*, June 1970 ("Di eytse," Feb 5, 1966)

"Fatal," *Cosmopolitan Magazine*, August 1973– ("Fatal," Mar 27, 28, 1970)

"Navon," *Jewish Chronicle*, September 13, 1974 ("Navon," Dec 21, 27, 1973)

"Mendel I Thought," *Playboy*, January 1977 ("'Peysakh kh'hob gemeynt,'" Jan 29, 30, 1976)

"Cat in Stockings," *Newsday Magazine*, 13 April 1986 (no known Yiddish publication)

"Job," *The New Yorker*, August 13, 2012 ("Iyev," May 22, 23, 29, 1970)

"Inventions," *The New Yorker*, January 26, 2015 ("Di temes," Act 16, 1965)

"The Gift of the Mishnah," *Tablet*, July 24, 2017 ("Mishnayes," *Goldene keyt*, 1960)

"A Window to the World," *Harper's*, January 2017 ("A fenster tsu der velt." Sep 16, 17, 23, 24, 30, 1976)

"The Final Gift," *Narrative*, Spring 2018 ("A matone," Feb 2, 3, 9, 1978)

"The Boarder," *The New Yorker*, May 7, 2018 (no known Yiddish publication)

"The Murderer," *The Paris Review*, Spring 2019 ("Der merder," *Tsukunft*, Jan 1972)

"A Letter to Mama," *The Jewish Review of Books*, Spring 2019 ("A brivele der mame'n," Oct 29, 30, Nov 5, 6, 1965)

"The Professor's Wife," *The American Scholar*, September 23, 2020 ("Di profesorshe," Sep 22, 1968)

"The Pass," *Literary Matters*, October 26, 2020 (no known Yiddish publication)

"Trio," *Jewish Renaissance*, January 2021 ("Dray," Aug 19, 25, 26, 1972)

"On a Ship," *The Sun Magazine*, February 2021 (no known Yiddish publication)

"Apudzhas Came to Say Goodbye," *Hey Alma*, June 22, 2021 ("Apudzhas is gekumen zikh gezegenen," Jan 22, 1976)

Printed in Dunstable, United Kingdom

64098707R00119